SIGN OF THE EIGHT

BENJAMIN LEBERT

SIGN OF THE EIGHT

Translation by Oliver Latsch

Arctis

W1-Media, Inc.
Arctis Books USA
Stamford, CT, USA

Copyright © 2022 by W1-Media Inc. for this edition
Text Copyright © 2020 by Benjamin Lebert
Im Zeichen der Acht first published in Germany by Arctis Verlag, 2020
First English language edition published by W1-Media Inc./Arctis, 2022

Visit our website at www.arctis-books.com

1 3 5 7 9 8 6 4 2

Library of Congress Control Number: 2 021 944 681
ISBN 978-1-64 690-009-1
ebook ISBN 978-1-64 690-609-3
Translation by Oliver Latsch
English translation edited by Carol Klio Burrell
Jacket design by Hauptmann & Kompanie Werbeagentur, Zürich

Printed in Germany, the European Union

MIX
Paper from
responsible sources
FSC
www.fsc.org   FSC® C083411

For Levi and for Claudia,
who filled a small chamber with light
and gave strength to a wavering heart.

PART ONE

THE
APPROACH

I

He followed the creature through the darkness into a band of spruce trees, where a steep aisle opened up in the forest. He was running fast. He could barely make out the uneven ground. He was lucky not to fall.

Paul's and the creature's footsteps echoed each other, and he felt as if their hearts were beating in sync, as well. As if there was nothing left that separated them, no boundaries of physical form. There was only the forest, the mystery of the night.

Suddenly a lake appeared behind the rows of tall tree trunks. The shard of moon, hovering at an icy height, cast a glimmer on the water.

This was remote Lake Flint, which even many of the locals never got up so far to see. It lay in a mountain basin within the Black Forest, surrounded by a mighty chain of hills. Coniferous trees lined its shores like an army of sentinels.

Paul, too, had never in his sixteen years of life seen it. He had heard stories told about it, though. Some people claimed that at its bottom sat the remains of a black fortress, home to a tyrannical ruler. Allegedly, the fortress had sunk centuries before in a flood that erupted from nearby Kyb Rock. Others said that there were hidden channels under the water connecting the basin lakes that had formed in the Ice Age.

Unlike those lakes, though, the waters of this lake were not acidic, and during the night you could see the shimmering bodies of fish darting out of the depths.

Paul paid no attention to the fish.

His senses were focused on the creature who had now stepped out from between conifers and onto the shore and was slowly turning to peer at him. Paul was still standing in the cover of the conifers, taking in the musty autumn scents. His eyes saw no more of the creature than the darkness that cloaked it and which barely stood out against the black surface of the lake. But the young man knew exactly who was there on the reedy shore ahead of him. His memory summoned the colors. Let him see without seeing: a robe made of many patches. The grimacing mask with the long, pointed nose and the gaping mouth from which the tongue stuck out. And he saw what was hidden under this mask carved from limewood and painted with a mixture of oil paints and linseed varnish—a second face.

It was the face of a young woman dressed in a witch's carnival costume. He knew her well. She was a student teacher at his school and had been attending classes for two months.

He knew her well. She showed up in his dreams.

He liked her eyes under her high, smooth forehead. There was a mystery in them and something demanding. As if there was a hunger gnawing at her. He liked the way she wore her hair. The plait with its braided and loose parts. And he liked the way her lips opened when she spoke in front of the class with a voice that sounded young and yet had the firmness of an aspiring teacher. He had imagined her resisting him but powerless. Imagined her voice losing that firmness and slowly melting into a moan.

Now there was no need for imagination, memories, and dreams. Now she was close. So close.

Around them, ferns, sedges, mosses, vines, the web of honey fungus that made the woods glow. Around them, the stirrings of the night creatures. The silent lapping of the water. Around them, nothing. The moment had come. At last he stepped out from between the trees and toward her.

～

She had led him here. He would never have believed it would be so easy. He had recognized her immediately by her voice. By the words: *Come with me.* He was sure: no one had noticed her disappearance. Quietly, in the distance, he could still hear drunk people chanting.

Twice a year, people from the surrounding villages climbed up to Kyb Rock to light a fire among the remains of a demolished castle. In spring to drive out the winter, and now on the night of the first of November. On that night, that fire was to carry sparks of life to the dead. That night, it was said, a crack opened. The gate that led into the realm of the dead.

Paul had also struck sparks into the night, as he had done since childhood. He had stuck a palm-size piece of wood onto the hazelnut stick he had cut earlier with his folding knife, which had a horn handle with leopardlike spots and which he always carried with him. He had set the wooden disk in the fire until it glowed and then swung the stick with the disk through the air. He had spoken the verse he had known since childhood. An old ritual. With that verse, the disks were consecrated. People cheered each time a disk was catapulted down the small slope into the valley.

Most of those who came to the ruins that night wore the costumes of the carnival guilds. Those were passed down through the generations and were usually worn during the parades in the spring, when witches and fools took over, village by village. But they were also worn on that special autumn night.

Paul did not wear a mask. He liked the feeling of being seen. He liked the feeling of people being exposed to his gaze. Liked seeing their uncertainty. It was the same with the young student teacher when he had first looked at her. She had not withstood the teenager's stare for long. He had felt acutely that his gaze had exposed something.

He stepped closer and closer to her on the shore. He knew now: they belonged to each other. Now he would know everything, sense by sense, layer by layer. The wooden mask fell off and the lips of this student teacher, whose first name he did not know, opened in the dark.

The patchwork robe dropped away. He felt himself get hard, blood coursing through him. He pulled down her panties.

She embraced him. With her body. Her breasts. Between her legs. Trapped him like a moth on the shore of the lake.

"What was that?" she said suddenly.

"What do you mean?" said Paul.

"There's something there. On the lake. A blue glow." Paul's eyes searched for it but couldn't spot anything.

Then they both heard it—a sound in the water.

"Just a fish, I'm sure," he said.

But what had detached itself from the lake's roots and was pushing its way out of the depths wasn't a fish. It was coming closer. Half swimming, half wading, it pulled itself to shore.

The two were spellbound. They could not move. The oozing creature rose up before them.

The creature resembled a human being. And yet was not a human.

Paul thought he saw pale, bloated flesh hanging from the bones. He thought he saw that the creature had empty eye sockets. The scrawny hand, covered with an oily coating, stretched toward the student teacher's face. Motionless, she crouched beside Paul on the narrow shore. Paul felt how quickly her chest rose and fell, how frantically she was breathing. His thoughts exhausted themselves. Was someone playing a trick on them? Was this also just someone in a carnival costume? He briefly thought of his folding knife, which was in his jeans pocket. He wanted to reach for it. But he couldn't, could not. He felt the nearness of the lake, he felt like was sinking into it. He felt soft, waving plants tangling around his limbs from the lake's bottom. He saw a sharp thumbnail slice the young woman's cheek. Blood gushed out, running down her face. Greedily, the creature licked the blood from its fingers.

It let the drops trickle into the warped opening of its mouth.

Those drops were only the beginning.

There were no screams. A tawny owl shot out of the spruces with a sound like tearing silk. Then silence fell again over Lake Flint, which carried away the flowing, un-fathomable images of the night.

2

Summer had long ago detached itself from the earth and gathered in its light. But the conifers, the omnipresent scowling conifers of the Black Forest, held on to their green.

Among these spruces and firs, which had always reached far up into the heights of her dreams, she walked.

She knew the path. Knew it well.

When Isabel reached a clear elevation, she could see the wooded areas all around, the ancient hills, and the sky, like clouded marble, in which darkness gathered.

Below her, she saw the lights of Hofsgrund, sparks of home and loathing. A hamlet of a few hundred inhabitants who lived at an altitude of over a thousand meters, below Schauinsland peak. A popular destination for hiking vacationers and skiers, Hofsgrund lay in the beautiful vastness of nature. But the inhabitants did not care for such immensity of thought.

Below her, Isabel could almost see in the distance the shingled roof of the house on Silberberg Street where she lived with other teenagers—the rebellious, the wayward.

The counselor, who was barely older than she, kept coming by to check on them. She acted like she belonged with them. As if she were a friend. On days when they were vulnerable, they believed her.

They were frequent, those days.

Isabel walked across the emaciated grass of a meadow and pushed deeper into the forest. The blues of the evening, the vines, creepers, and twigs became an ever finer web. Isabel had to hurry. The supervisor had made it clear, with a stern face, what time she expected Isabel to be back.

Once before, Isabel had run away and spent more than a day up here in the open, until a search party had trooped out and brought her back. She remembered that day well. The sounds that had gradually grown louder and more intense—the rustling, the clawing, the scratching. She remembered the movement of unseen wings and the slight stirrings of air. The quietly gnawing hunger. The plants that grew so slowly that you were afraid of them, because you couldn't guess what they were up to. She had eaten some of the plants, even though she didn't have a clue which ones were poisonous. She remembered one plant in particular, elongated and narrow, growing out into the sky from a clearing. Afterward, Isabel had gotten stomach cramps. Nothing more had happened. But she still had stomach cramps far too frequently and each time, she tasted that plant on her tongue. Time had slipped on as if in a dream.

Nevertheless, she had felt free for the first time in a long time.

In fact, Isabel was no longer allowed to go into the forest alone. But today was an exception. Today was a special day. A day that all the other children and teenagers around her associated with Halloween. The ancient Celts had called it Samhain, the night of the first of November, when many a boundary was supposedly mysteriously lifted.

Isabel knew her way, knew it well.

She had no idea that something was emerging from earthy depths.

Coming closer and closer.

⌒

The little chapel of St. Margaret lay hidden deep in the forest. No marked path led there. Some hikers who had set out to find it returned in the evening with the tale of their failure. The forest buried the chapel in its heart.

Isabel had read about it in the bookshop of the local history museum. Christian Albert, an old man she visited every week, had taken her there once.

It was not as boring as she had expected. There was also something in another book about the chapel. A settlement that had once existed there had been destroyed long ago. At that time, in the 19th century, the timber trade had flourished and the silver firs had been cut down and made into masts for Dutch ships of war and trade. The forest had almost disappeared, and the livelihood of the inhabitants was threatened. The state of Baden claimed the lands for itself to reforest them. Many farmers were forced to give up their properties.

But the small chapel resisted the centuries and remained standing.

There was a legend, from faraway times when the plague had ravaged through the Black Forest valleys. According to the legend, only places where the bells of St. Margaret's could be heard were spared from the pestilence.

When Isabel stepped into the chapel, she was met by damp coolness. She lit a sacrificial candle. Its light spread hesitantly, and it could barely overcome the deepening darkness. Little by little, the colors of the stained glass vanished.

Isabel stared into the candleflame and felt like her body was evaporating into the night. She consisted of only a face, floating weightlessly in the musty air, looking outward, eyes fixed on the flame. For a brief moment, she thought she heard singing, a kind of choir. Then it was silent again.

In the tenuous light of the candle, she knelt with her hands folded, as if she were praying. But she wasn't praying. She was trying to think of her mother.

Every year on her mother's birthday, Isabel lit a candle here. But the images that surfaced in her mind were not of her mother. They were images of other women she had met fleetingly. Women she sometimes stealthily followed on the street because something about them reminded her of her mother. The build, the wavy hair, a hint of perfume. Isabel always tried to avoid looking at the women's faces so that the sweet illusion would endure. But then she did. These women were alive and went on their way. But her mother, she was dead.

When Isabel came back out into the air, the moon was in the sky, like a shimmering notch that had been carved into the night. She stopped in front of the chapel and breathed in the cold air. She adjusted the collar of her coat, which was too thin for this time of the year. She liked it, though, because she felt sexy in it, and it contrasted perfectly with her blond hair.

Isabel suddenly thought of Daniel, whom she always met when she rode her bike to the farm to buy eggs. He was sixteen—the same age as her—and was in a different homeroom. His father owned the farm. When she went there, the young man always looked at her with such wonder. Her friends all said he was much too well-behaved. Boring. But Isabel liked his gentle face. Very much. It wasn't locked shut, like the faces of other boys. It revealed a lot. You could tell he came from a world that was clearly defined, one that smelled of buttercups, hay, and cow manure. You could tell he was more interested in things rooted in the earth than images that gleamed on touchscreens. But that's precisely what she liked about him.

✆

The tree that Isabel often stood and gazed at stood in the moonlight—a hanging beech which stood to the left of the chapel in a small clearing, its somber tangle of small and large branches sprawled almost to the ground. For a brief moment her gaze was caught in the tangle.

Then Isabel heard a sound.

At first, she thought she heard only the wind blowing through the forest. Then she realized that it was most definitely not the wind. It was a soft gurgling groan like a strained breath that wouldn't let up. The sound came from the depths. From the depths of the disused, half-ruined well that sat halfway between the hanging beech and the chapel. The sound seemed to swell in the well's shadows, coming nearer and nearer.

Isabel scurried behind the promontory of the chapel's walls.

Her breathing was shallow and rapid. She peered over at the well and saw what was emerging from the shaft.

She saw hands, a body silhouetted against the darkness, pushing out into the open. Isabel heard the pulsing of her blood in her ears. A naked creature with sore, charred flesh rolled from the well's ledge down to the grass. Isabel did not dare to move. Her eyes no longer wanted to look but did so anyway. She saw the body crawl laboriously forward across the ground. She heard the labored breathing, which sounded different from that of a human being. Almost as if this being had to painfully learn to breathe. There was rustling and cracking in the grass as the creature crawled along. It crawled toward the hanging beech and disappeared behind the curtain of hanging branches. There it remained, breathing. Breathing.

Isabel wanted to run away. But she couldn't. Something tied her to that place. What had slipped into the shadows there seemed to have forged an invisible bond with her.

She cautiously approached the tree, which seemed enchanted in the blue of the night. When she reached it, she stopped, hesitated. Fear still surged through her body. But then she took heart. She felt the touch of fine twig tips as she slipped under the hanging branches.

There under the tree trunk in the dim light lay no longer a flame-consumed creature but the body of a huddled, naked woman, with curls around her pale face. She looked up at Isabel from the leaf-covered earth. Her trembling hands reached out to her in a gesture seeking help. Isabel thought she saw a vein protruding from her pale forehead. Then the young woman grabbed her hand and bit furiously into her flesh. Isabel cried out. The woman immediately let go of her. It seemed as if she was frightened by her own act. She sank back to the earth, making helpless movements as if she wanted to dissolve into the darkness. Her fingers clawed at the dead foliage, which offered no purchase.

Isabel turned away, wanted to run away as quickly as possible. But she did not move. She had the strong sense that she could not detach herself from this woman. She could not leave her behind.

Despite the laws of nature, it seemed to her that the brightness of the day was returning, in red and orange colors.

Isabel looked down at the naked stranger and thought she perceived it in her eyes: the glow. Then Isabel heard the woman's brittle voice.

"You have to help me," she said.

3

C hristian Albert sat at his workbench and suspected nothing.

He was busy lathing a palm-size wooden disk that would later become a wheel with fifty teeth. An essential part of a mechanical balance-beam Waagbalken clock, which he was making according to the old Black Forest tradition. He built these clocks in different shapes and sizes. One after another, with aging, battered hands that possessed the calmness so essential to this work. With a heart that did not know rest.

In his youth, he had apprenticed as a precision mechanic. His years in the factory had been filled with the roar of machines and the screech of steel meeting steel.

The incomparably quiet work with pliant wood had become an indispensable hobby for him.

Christian Albert strictly adhered to the old watchmaking customs that had fascinated him since childhood. He cut the wood for his clocks only on the nights between Christmas and New Year's Day, during waning moons. The blanks for the gears lay in liquid manure for four weeks and afterward hung outside in his smoke chamber, between hams and sausages, until they became black and hard and could not be warped. The machines with which he ground, drilled, and turned had all been built by him-

self from wood. Most were driven by foot, by steady trea-
dling.

Christian Albert sat at his workbench and suspected
nothing . . .

❧

The workshop he had built out of beams from a demolished farm was adjacent to the small forester's house he
had lived in since his wife's death. He had inherited it from
his grandparents when he was still a teenager. For a long
time, the forester's house had been a retreat for vacations.
After his wife's death, he had left their Hofsgrund pent-
house south of the Schauinsland summit.

The forester's house, which lay a few forest-cloaked
miles down the valley from the village, had turned into his
only residence. A leaf-covered home in the middle of the
forest, on the edge of civilization.

At first, he had felt uneasy in its seclusion. Then he
had gotten used to it. Working on his watches helped
him.

But after his wife died, something had happened. He
had become unable to stand the ticking that had been a
source of comfort to him for so many years. So he only
made clocks that remained silent, with hands that did not
move. Christian Albert made clocks that silenced time.
Many of them decorated the walls of the cottage and the
workshop. Many clocks. One silence.

He sat at the workbench and suspected nothing . . .

Outside the windowpane covered with gossamer wood
shavings, the sun had turned to blood. Blackness now lay

over the autumnal forest. He saw sparse lights from his left-behind world, shimmering tiny and distant.

Inside, an oil lamp cast its glow over the countertop, over the drill, and the chair. And over the fur of his dog, Nina, who was dozing on the floor, occasionally making whimpering sounds of dreaming.

As these sounds drifted into his subconscious along with the familiar sounds of his work, he thought of his wife. Tatjana. She had suffered from an eye disorder. As she had grown older, her days had gradually disappeared behind a veil. He thought of how her delicate fingers had run along the walls of the loft, groping for a path. Those fingers had known all the irregularities of each surface. Had sensed edges, dangerous pitfalls. Only once had the fingers failed in their duty, on a day in March when he had not been home. An unfortunate fall, they had called it.

Several months had passed since then.

He went twice a week to her grave in the hillside cemetery. He would leave Nina at home. He took his folding chair with him because he couldn't stand for long, and a woolen blanket. His wife had knitted it for him more than half a century past. As a young woman, knitting had been her support after losing their child—their only child, who had stopped living two hours and twenty-three minutes after birth.

He would put the blanket over his lap when he sat at the graveside, feeling the heaviness and warmth of all those years against his legs. When it rained, he would simply open an umbrella while he sat by the grave.

Lately, he often dreamed of his wife. He heard her voice

saying: *Help the girl!* At first, he had thought she meant the child they had lost. But now he was no longer sure.

Christian Albert did not know who she could be referring to.

He was pondering this when Nina snapped him out of his thoughts. She had suddenly risen from the floor. Her big head with its deep eyes and long snout was directed at the closed door. Her nose sniffed something. The sharply erect ears listened outside, into the darkness. Christian Albert smiled as he looked at her. He was very fond of his mongrel dog, whose existence expressed all the contradictions of life and also the ability not to be affected by them in any way.

Christian Albert stopped smiling when he heard the footsteps approaching the workshop. The footsteps and the heavy breathing.

The old man stood up and quietly extinguished the oil lamp so he could see better through the window whatever was going on outside. That hope quickly faded.

Outside, only the dark shroud of the night was visible.

He tentatively opened the window a crack. Cold air burst through in eddies.

Meanwhile, the footsteps were coming closer. Someone was on his property. Was outside in the garden, in front of the door. Their breathing sounded unnaturally loud. Briefly, he saw a glimmer of light under the crack of the door. It was a strangely warm hue, like the evening glow of the sun. However, the sun had long since disappeared into the darkness.

Nina, who had up until then remained motionless, started to pace around the narrow space in the workshop. Panting, she trotted toward the door, returned to him, then approached the door again. This went on a few times. She did not bark, however. No whimpering, no signs of fear. Only a restlessness like tense anticipation.

On a spring night when some lowlife had gained access to the property to get drunk, Nina had barked into the sky as if she could chase away the grey shadow of the rabbit in the moon. Now she made no sound.

Then there was a knock at the door, not very loud. A voice, not very loud.

"Mr. Albert, please open up!" Christian Albert knew the voice. It belonged to Isabel from the group home where the young people lived. The ones who had it hard or made it hard for others, depending on how you looked at it.

Isabel had never made it hard for him. She was polite. Quiet. He liked to share the silence with her. Never had he thought that something could grow in that silence that would put him in danger.

$\backsim$

Isabel came to see him once a week. She would lend a hand where it was needed, help him run errands. They cooked together. Sometimes they played cards. He had taught her Cego, a game from Baden he had known since childhood and used to play with his wife. Actually, you couldn't play as a pair. You needed several people to play it. But he had come up with a more straightforward version where you only needed one player. Isabel's favorite card was the poke, the highest ranking card. Mr. Albert liked the smile that appeared when she saw it. A smile that showed a crooked tooth.

Isabel's counselor had made the arrangements. She thought these visits would do her good. Connecting with life, she called it. But he was an old man. You were much more likely to come in contact with death being around him, he thought.

Isabel had never come to visit so late, or unannounced.

He opened the door of the workshop. Christian Albert saw that she was not alone. Someone was with her, out there—a slender figure.

"Please!" he invited them, because they couldn't seem to get their mouths open. Hesitantly, he asked her to step over his threshold.

∾

He could not immediately make out the person Isabel was bringing into the workshop. Only when the light of the oil lamp was reignited did he see that it was a young woman, scarcely older than Isabel. She seemed barely able to stand on her feet. Isabel supported the petite, swaying body. The other young woman's hair was curly, and she possessed a mysterious beauty that seemed to him like the memory of an irretrievable bliss. But her eyes, the young woman's eyes, seemed as if they had stared into an abyss.

She was wearing a thin coat that he knew belonged to Isabel. Underneath, the woman appeared to be naked. He saw battered skin, a pitch-black belly button. He detected the tinge of a musty smell that reminded him of the nuns' crypt he had once seen on a tour of Freiburg's hidden vaulted cellars. He saw the woman's dirty feet and her hands, groping for a handhold, with blood-crusted nails. Nina, who usually gleefully pounced on Isabel to lick her face, stayed back. He had never seen such an expression on her canine face. He thought he recognized awe, although he wasn't sure a dog could feel such a thing. Nina timidly approached the woman now, licking her fingers as if to soothe a pain. Only gradually was Christian Albert able to sort out his thoughts.

"What is this?" he said to Isabel. "Who are you dumping on me?" Isabel told him she had found the woman in that condition in the woods. That something terrible must have happened to her. That she was confused. She wouldn't even give her name.

"She seems to be afraid of something," Isabel said. "Someone—something—is after her."

"Who? Who is after you?" asked Christian Albert the woman. She didn't answer. She looked at him, just looked at him . . . He wanted to scold Isabel for bringing the poor creature here, of all places. To him. Tell her that he wanted nothing to do with this. Then he caught another glance from his dog. Christian Albert knew that glance and could seldom resist it. A look that was like a silent plea. His resentment found no more words. He smiled, let himself become gentle and composed. His mind was working. He said he would call a doctor and notify the police.

The woman became visibly agitated. In a forceful voice, she said, "No tracks, no. Leave no trail." That was all he could get out of her.

Suddenly he thought of the displaced persons from the war.

A few of them had shown up then, with chapped feet and no belongings, in the small Black Forest town where he had grown up.

Among them had been a girl, five years old. He had still been a baby when she arrived. But a time when he was to tenderly whisper her name was soon to come. Tatjana.

Christian Albert looked at the pale woman standing barefoot in his workshop. Finally, he gave in and led the two of them come through. Nina followed them. Fearfully, the stranger, supported by Isabel, peered around. The moon was haunting the trees.

They entered the small cottage, which consisted of a single long room divided into kitchen, sleeping, and living areas. He had Isabel pick out a cotton dress that had belonged to his wife for the stranger from a dresser. It was the only garment of hers that he had kept. Her lily perfume still clung ever so faintly to it. The dress was too tight for the young woman, in certain places. He tried to ignore how her nipples stood out under the fabric. At least now she had something to clothe her body. She also received some slippers, and he gave her his cardigan so that she would be warmer.

Isabel said goodbye with the promise to come back the next day after school to check on her. It had gotten very late. Isabel would have been expected back at the group home a long time ago. Then he and Nina were alone with the stranger.

She sat on the bed. Cautiously, the dog approached her and began to sniff her fingers. The young woman calmly let Nina have her hand. Then she began to scratch the dog under the chin with one finger.

"You should eat something," Christian Albert said. "You need to get your strength back." The old man didn't own a refrigerator. A hinged door in the floor opened to a tiny cool storage space for food, and a few other, useful features in case of trouble, which he had made mouse-proof. A small ladder led down. He rummaged around to see what he had in there. He was not practiced at entertaining and generally struggled with cooking. What food to serve someone who had obviously had something terrible happen to them? He decided on brown bread with bibilis cheese, a Black Forest soft cheese made of low-fat curds and sweet cream, and topped with chives, onions, and spices. He pressed the curd through a hair sieve to loosen it, just like Tatjana had always done. He served it with sauerkraut, which he cooked with plenty of butter. Soon the distinctive heavy smell of the heated cabbage spread through the cottage. But the stranger could hardly manage a bite. She stared ahead of her, with eyes that were open and yet seemed to be in the grip of dark dreams.

He let her have his bed. Nina stayed there with her in the house. He prepared a place for himself to sleep in the workshop.

He took a book of old Black Forest legends with him, well-worn because he loved to read in it.

His sinewy fingers turned many pages during that night because he couldn't sleep. However, he could not read either. The letters slipped away from him, and he found himself in the emptiness that lay between the lines.

His thoughts wandered in ways that made him uneasy. Where did the woman come from? Was it right to give her shelter? What did those words mean? *Leave no trail.* A strange phrase. As if fallen out of another time.

Toward morning, when a light sleep finally fell over him, he heard his wife's voice again.

Protect the girl!

He startled awake, drenched in sweat. He felt that something was coming closer—closer and closer. Something he was powerless against.

From what? What was he supposed to protect this girl from?

4

Threads of sunlight filtered through the trees as he set to work. The light of the afternoon was somewhat ephemeral and had the color of overripe apricots. In contrast, he sensed a beginning. A beginning that was like the opening of a blade.

A night and half a day had passed, there by the lake. The blood and flesh of the two young people had nourished him. He felt his strength returning. His life force. And how inner currents arose to sustain him. How tendons and nerves connected, in this body in which a wrathful will ruled, directed toward a single indelible goal. From within the body, the name surged forth onto his tongue. The name that had been submerged for so many years. A name of darkness: Nightsworn. Tristan Nightsworn.

Images emerged from memory. The battlefields on which he had fought, the rivers of red that had seeped into the cracks of the earth, from where they brought forth—so the people used to say—the glow of new days. Tristan felt that glow. And how it spread through him.

A particular vision also came back to him: the image of a woman with whose fate he was inextricably linked.

Tristan knew that she had also already returned. He felt her near. Although he could not determine exactly where she was. Not yet. He sensed her presence like the delicate scent of a flower. He would find her soon. He knew his purpose.

⟜

He had done well. Had left the two bodies lying exposed for now so that the scent would attract other animals. A fox, roaming the barren expanses of autumn, had approached cautiously. But its caution had not saved it. He had broken its neck. As Tristan Nightsworn had sunk his teeth into the raw flesh, he had lapsed into a state that had come close to the strongest feelings he had ever felt. Then he had sunk into sleep, deep and unknowing. Afterward, he had picked up the jackknife that had found in the young man's pants, which were made of a blue, very sturdy fabric. He had never seen such legwear before. But he did not pause to wonder about it. Everything had a naturalness to it. As if, to his eyes, which were seeing ever more clearly, the tremendous changes brought about by this new age were no more than the barely perceptible change over a day in the angle of light.

He felt safe. He felt energy pulsing through him and his senses reaching into regions he had never even imagined before. He registered them: the life impulses out there in the vastness. He experienced a sense of majesty over them. Even a feeling of being able to control them, to harness them for his own purpose. And above all, he felt them giving him direction: his task.

The day was waning. Colors faded, darkness came.

The time had come. He took the human skins he had previously dried on branches and wrapped them around him like a protective covering. He felt their weight, the little weight that remained of life. He waded into the lake, plunged into its darkness. When he emerged from the water a little later, he wore a coat that was an intense blue color.

Soft and supple, the coat closed around his slender body.

⮑

Tristan climbed upslope to a limestone outcrop that jutted from the forest like the bow of a petrified ship. From there, he looked down into the valley, where the lights of the Freiburg suburb of Günterstal glowed. With his superfine senses, he heard the voices from below like a whispering wind in his ears. Felt the restlessness of human heartbeats. His eyes widened, searching until his gaze found entrance into houses and dreams. They found what they were looking for. Hidden in an alley was the window of a tiny store. Tristan smiled. Like the other stores, the shop had already closed, but a dim light burned inside. His senses registered a man sitting behind a counter inside. Behind him were dusty glass shelves that took up the entire back of the store. Tristan liked it, this store. He liked what he could find there. And he liked the man who sat there with his sweaty rough hands, thinking his thoughts. Which were groundless and gloomy. So gloomy and despicable.

Tristan Nightsworn smiled.

5

The first night after her return flowed by like a dark stream. She slept.

For a short time, she thought she was sinking back into the sleep of death, in which the word, the meaning "I" disappeared so quietly and only a spark of consciousness strayed toward where there were frenzy, voices, and lights. Sometimes, it seemed to her that a new life had emerged from that spark for a little while. A path had opened that she did not know.

She had been a stranger on this path. Until the foreign face had become her own. Little by little, the face had dissolved again and disappeared. Sleep had reigned again while they reached for her, the sounds of the world to which she no longer belonged. A world that always seemed to be near and yet unreachable. She remembered the pounding of machines, the sound of destructive weaponry, which differed from the sound of the swords she had once known and wielded herself.

They sounded far more powerful than the bolts of a crossbow hurtling through the air. More powerful than the balls of flame hurled by catapults and the fire-spreading wreaths of pitch. Louder than the banging shots of the blunderbuss and the thud of the trebuchet pots filled with black powder, sulfur, saltpeter, broken glass, and lead.

Only the screams sounded the same as they always had.

Gradually, she had become aware of the spreading roar. She remembered feeling the piercing glint of colors. The tremendous, spreading greed of people. Of images that were inexhaustible and made her nerves tingle.

And suddenly, there was a voice, growing louder. A voice that called her back. And with it came the memory of the body she had belonged to, once. The body of a young woman. She began to feel it again, to enter into it. But that also brought back the images of the men removing her shackles, only to tear the clothes from her body. She felt again how a merciless hand had dragged her out of the rear of the chapel that had been Martha's hiding place. Saw again how a curtain was pulled back and the instruments revealed. The stool she was forced down onto was hard. But as her hands lay on the tin-covered table under the iron clamp, and her joints were immobilized with iron shackles, and the pain began, the wood of the stool under her buttocks became the only sensation that was bearable. She tried to concentrate on it, but the pain, the raging pain, had been the sole ruling sensation. Afterward, there was not even a stool to sit on as she stood naked, gasping against a pillar, her wrists tied with tight cords to an iron hook, as the whip of hazel rods struck her and the blood ran down her back.

And then there was the sensation of the little unborn being that had been growing in this body of hers and had been given over to the flames. She felt the flames, their greed far surpassing even the greed of humans. She felt the distant sensation of a love that had turned into frenzy and had summoned the enemy she now had to confront.

The night smothered the fire. She had seen the sky break into seven shards that had crashed down on her. Beast-like creatures emerged from the shards. True beasts. Each one had looked different. She, too, was transformed into a creature. She was the eighth of them. The beasts fell upon each other to tear each other apart.

When the sleep of death ended, she had felt again the task that had been given to her so long ago, that had been inscribed in her heart. She knew the moment had dawned when this task must be accomplished.

⌒

The night's sleep she now experienced in the old man's house was different. The images were not as piercing. The blackness was not so deep. Instead, everything seemed closer, more present—even the peace.

She enjoyed the warmth of the woodstove the old man had lit for her before he had gone out to sleep in the work-shop.

When she opened her eyes, she saw the dog had been keeping watch by her bedside, its head tucked between her front legs. She had felt the presence of it all night long. The animal seemed to perceive where she had come from. Although it sensed the danger that accompanied her appearance, the animal was not afraid of her. The realms of death seemed familiar to the dog.

As if from that realm, scents wafted to her constantly from the deep forest that surrounded the house.

The hunger that the young—in truth, not at all young—woman felt was terrible. Because it could not be easily satiated and found nothing else to consume, she felt like it had already begun to devour her soul.

She had to take care not to pounce on the animal. She perceived the flow of the dog's blood. She felt her own need, the greed. She craved clear currents of nature, not food that had already been stripped of its life force and cooked to be palatable, like the meal the old man had served her yesterday. As she crawled out of bed, she struggled to stay on her feet.

She looked out the window and saw a new day dawning, for the very first time after a seemingly interminable amount of time. Her body was almost not strong enough for this happiness.

She pushed the window open. Breathed deep, breathed in the tart air of autumn. Woodlands faded into a smoky blue distance. Fog rose from valleys and hollows, billowed over the treetops. Life out there walked on silent soles. Only a crow wanted to be heard. It was beautiful. So beautiful.

⌒

Christian Albert trod into the house with the slow steps of his age. Nina came up to him, wagging her tail, and pushed her nose between his knees in a gesture of trust. The old man took her big head between his hands and tickled her with his thumbs behind her fluffy ears.

He fed the dog and lit wood in the kitchen stove's firebox, the flames pushing against the glass in its door.

The old man said nothing to the woman, but he smiled at her. He seemed quite tall. That was striking. Everything in this new time she found herself in seemed more immense, more sprawling than the things she knew. Also cleaner, purer somehow. Hardly any filth on them, no ever-present plague lying in wait.

At first, the smells had seemed to her a little weaker, more mellowed.

Then she noticed that this was not so. Something hung in the atmosphere like dust. Like mischief. Her senses were awake. They were traveling long distances, opening doors. She was surprised how much she could make out. She did not judge. Her duty was not to judge. Her duty was to act. In the short amount of time that she had. Otherwise, soon there would no longer be a world to judge at all.

She marveled at how easy it was for her to settle into this new present, which was nothing like the one she had once known. It was as if she had just woken up from a brief episode of unconsciousness and simply needed a few breaths to get her bearings again. Yes, it almost seemed as if she belonged here. Almost.

Often, though, her vision faded. She felt that she had nowhere near enough strength to push her senses to any significant degree. To see what needed to be seen. To do what needed to be done.

"What's your name?" the old man asked suddenly, taking a pan from the hook on the wall. "Aren't you going to tell me?"

Out of the deep murmur in her head came the name. She heard it pass her lips—the name she had carried in a long-lost time.

"Martha von Falkenstein."

"Well, Martha von Falkenstein," he said, "my name is Christian." He pointed to the dog. She had devoured her meal and then fervently drunk an entire bowl of water. After that culinary distraction, she now seemed alert again, watching them as a long thread of drool trailed from the corner of her mouth.

He melted butter in the pan under the heat of the stove. "And the lady who stayed with you last night is named Nina." He had brought a carton from the pantry and set it on the countertop. Six raw eggs were inside. Martha grabbed two of them when he wasn't looking, bit the shells, and swallowed the contents. The old man's eyes darted back to her. He saw the eggshells still clinging to her hands and the slippery egg white hanging around her mouth, dripping in threads from her fingertips.

Glancing at Nina, who was licking up dripped egg from the floor, Christian Albert said, "You two seem to have a lot in common."

After breakfast, Martha had to lie down again. She couldn't manage to stay on her feet. The old man fetched several blankets and used them to provide a little more warmth. Then he withdrew so as not to disturb her. Said he wanted to go over to the workshop.

He put on his jacket and opened the door. "Do you want to come, Nina?" Usually, before he even asked, the dog would start wagging her tail and barking happily. Then she would push past him to get out into the open first. Usually. Now, she did nothing of the sort. She lay on the floor in front of the bed, not taking her eyes off the young woman.

"Deal. You stay here and keep an eye on Martha."

Martha lay still on the bed. Time passed.

She heard a fine rain falling outside. Then everything was quiet. Too quiet.

Disturbing thoughts came.

She had to satiate herself. Breakfast had been only a touch of life.

Not enough by a long stretch.

She was going to have to be strong. But she was nowhere near strong enough.

She was aware of that. She had to ingest something. A food that could have a kindling effect, to give her the strength she needed.

She felt his presence. The man who knew no mercy . . . At one point, it seemed to her that he was near the house. As if he was already lurking out there in the haze of the day.

The first eight days. That was the period in which he could do her harm. She had to survive these eight days. Then she would be safe. At least for the time being.

She didn't know if he had already started to choose the people who would stand by him. Who there would fight by his side? Time was running out fast. She didn't know if he had acquired it yet—his sword. The thought of it made her feel desperate.

He would also try to seize the second sword. *Her* sword. But it had not returned to this world. Not yet.

In her mind she saw the two swords in front of her.

Two swords, forged in a monastic workshop eight centuries ago under the spring moon, just before a mighty, noisy human procession finally set out into the unknown after a grueling wait—to reclaim the land that was called holy, was supposed to bestow holiness . . . where, in truth, only death awaited.

The procession at that time had included the bishop Thomas Olivier and his advisors, knights and squires, scattered children, the more-or-less orderly ranks of the foot-soldiers, archers, and spearmen. The entourage: carpenters and blacksmiths, merchants with carts, barbers and field doctors, whose carts contained not only tinctures but also the charms of light-spirited young women. In addition, there were jugglers, minstrels, and singers.

In the midst of this inexorably advancing mass, there moved a woman and a man who never seemed to be apart. Each carried a sword. The swords belonged together in the way that only love can bring beings and things together.

The man's sword was called Xanas. Aurin was the name of the woman's sword.

The swords were baptized many weeks later in a distant land under a scorching sun that peeled off layer after layer of skin from the warriors. The swords were baptized in blood. Martha remembered it well.

Martha's thoughts lost their foothold, exhausted. She was too tired to drive them onward. Too weak to follow them. Yet, she had to concentrate. Focus on where it would appear in this new present.

Aurin, her sword.

She saw a girl before her with hair the color of sunset. The girl was Keth, her sister. Had been. At that time.

Martha had given the sword to Keth before she had hidden in a chapel called St. Margaret's. Before she had been found there and in the end had been reduced to a charred body thrown down the well.

Keth worked her days on a spoil heap in front of the rocks where miners dug narrow tunnels searching for galena in the damp darkness. She worked alongside the other scavengers—children, infirm men, and old women. All day long, she hewed the rock brought to the surface, separating the waste from the silver. But when evening came, Keth would steal away. Deep into the forest.

There was a charcoal burner there whom she loved. From a distance, she would hear the sounds he raised from his *hillebille*, an instrument the charcoal burners used to signal one another. They communicated with its resonant sounds of clapper against crossbeam.

When he kissed her, he left black soot on her skin. One evening Keth gave this charcoal burner Martha's sword, which had been her burden and source of fear. The charcoal-burner hid the blade sunk deep into his charcoal pile.

Martha saw all this now. She saw it with firmly closed eyes even as she felt the closeness of her adversary. Before he took it, the sword had to find its way back to her. She had a vague idea how this was possible. She tried to bring small fragments from her dream into reality.

Time was running out.

6

They appeared. In the dim light of the store. In the dim light of his thoughts: all the schoolgirls. With their soft, young bodies and flushed faces. Their eyes filled with innocence and with what was slowly beginning to consume that innocence: lust. He knew they could not resist it.

In his mind's eye, he saw the girls. Saw their legs under the fluttering skirts that sometimes showed too much. A tremor came over him at the thought.

Briefly, the image of a particular girl detached itself from the swirl of bodies. He thought he remembered that her name began with the letter *L*. She had once crossed against the light on her bicycle. He had reprimanded her. As was his duty. As a policeman. As a good, *good* policeman. That's how they had met. He had then accompanied her on her way to school, for her safety, of course. A few times, that was how it had gone. He waited for her at the corner of the street. He was diligent.

It was obvious to him. The girls twirled their hair. They liked him—the policeman, tall, athletic, twenty-five years old. They liked him a lot. Obviously they would.

Then he saw the look on the girl's face when he had opened his pants. He hadn't touched her. Of course he hadn't. He wasn't stupid, after all. He had to be careful. He

couldn't afford to make the slightest mistake in his honor-
able service of protecting the public. But the expression on
her face had been enough. More than enough.

He liked these evenings when he had time off and was
by himself. He liked to sit in the store in the side street in
this godforsaken Guenter Valley and let himself be carried
away by his thoughts. He liked the various implements for
fishing. But more than that, he liked the variety of weapons that could be bought here. Rifles for hunting. Revolv-
ers for self-defense. The long knives. Tobis' Fishing and
Gun Store was the name of the store. With a misplaced
apostrophe. He had brought that up a couple of times, to
no avail. Ever since the store existed, the bad apostrophe
had belonged to it like a splinter lodged under the skin that
would never work its way out.

The store belonged to his brother. He and his brother
lived in the yellow, very narrow building they had inherited on the corner of the street. On two floors. That was all
there was. He lived upstairs. The brother and his indolent
bitch of a wife lived on the ground floor, where the store
was.

In the evening, the ground floor was usually deserted.
The others were gone. Separately, of course. His brother
went off with people to Freiburg town center to drink. The
indolent bitch of a wife went off to her sister's, where they
stuffed chips into themselves with the TV on and they gos-
siped about how terrible his brother was.

He sat behind the dusty counter. At his back, the
glass-fronted shelves with more expensive items rose to
the ceiling. He sat and watched as dusk turned to night
outside. He had what he needed. Finely crafted utensils

that brought death; thoughts of young fluttering birds that made him feel the heat of life.

His fingers began to rub at his fly, when suddenly a bluish light appeared in the semi-darkness of the store. A man appeared, wearing a strange coat. He had entered unnoticed. The store had been closed for over an hour, and the policeman had lowered the grate. Had he forgotten to lock the rear door to the backyard? Had he made it easy for an intruder? He had never been so goddamn careless before.

"Beautiful weapons," the stranger said in a flattering voice. But he wasn't looking at the shelves. He was looking at him.

The policeman, sensing danger, did not hesitate. He swung his big, muscular body out of the chair and jumped over the counter, determined to grab the guy. He was skilled at immobilizing people. Most of the time, it happened so fast they didn't even notice. Before they knew it, they were overpowered, wriggling helplessly. But just as he was about to strike, the intruder plunged a knife into his flesh below the right shoulder. The policeman felt the pain, the gushing blood. His vision began to waver. He fell to the ground.

He was not used to losing control or being at someone's mercy. He even felt something he was only familiar with from hearsay, a thing that moved frantically from place to place, body to body. It called itself fear.

"Beautiful weapons," repeated the stranger with the strange coat. "Beautiful birds."

"What the hell are you talking about?" Dully, he took note of how the man leaned down toward him. How his lips opened close to his ear.

"You know very well what I mean. Glorious, the way they flutter about. In the streets and skies. Here in the store. In there in your head." A sharp fingernail touched his temple.

No, this wasn't going to be a burglary! This had to be someone with a daughter. A father who might have overheard something and now was here to get even. The policeman had been careful. But maybe not careful enough. With great effort, he managed to move. His hand groped for the pistol he carried in the holster on his belt.

But then the stranger yanked him up into the air and hurled him over the counter against the glass display cases. The policeman registered the resounding crash as the glass shattered. But at first, he did not know that it was he who had crashed through the glass. But then he felt the splinters that drilled into his back. Where his pistol had gone, he did not know.

He sank to the floor beside the counter.

From there, he looked up at the stranger. His mind was still awake, though his body was weakening, and he was struggling to keep his eyes open. The stranger's skin stretched over his distinctive face, so thin that one could see all the bones beneath. But a dark power seemed to emanate from this man, like light from a lamp. The policeman was no match for this power. It came from a source as deep as hatred, as black as night. And suddenly, a feeling stirred in him that was even stronger than the feeling of his helplessness: admiration for this being. For its strength and ruthlessness, which seemed unstoppable. He had never experienced anything like it before.

"I know what you're capable of," he heard the man's voice say. "I know what you're after. I like them, your dreams. That's the only reason I'll let you live. For a little while. Until the time is right." He rammed the knife, which had a horn handle and had greasy blood clinging to its blade, into the wood of the counter. There it stuck, trembling gently for a few seconds. The stranger's eyes, that were staring at him now! It seemed as if they wanted to unleash something. Something that was hidden deep under his skin. The policeman was still lying on the ground, but suddenly he didn't feel pain anymore. He felt only the happiness that sprang from evil deeds and never dried up, flowing through centuries.

"Who are you?" the policeman asked.

"You don't need to know my name. I'm here to collect something." A slender index finger with a sharpened nail pointed to the glass case above the counter. There, where the glass had fractured, was a sword resting horizontally in a stand made of wood. It was a double-edged, sharply ground longsword. It belonged to the policeman's brother and was not for sale. It was only for display. His brother had a thing for the Middle Ages. He'd had the sword specially made by a blacksmith, and it had cost half a fortune.

The stranger's gaunt, emaciated hand approached the sword and closed around its hilt. He took the sword, held it up to the light, looked at it with an appraising gaze.

Then the stranger moved away from the counter, coat billowing around him. This is no ordinary man, the policeman thought, with pride. With pride at having met this stranger.

Then the stranger slipped out of his field of vision. Disappeared into the vast darkness that now fell upon the policeman.

7

Christian Albert's mind would not settle down. He sensed that Martha was in danger, but he did not know who or what was threatening her.

He did not know what to do. What could he—an old man—do? Care for her, yes, that he could. But would he also be able to protect her? The young woman might have done something wrong. Maybe something terrible, something that could hardly be forgiven.

Was it right to protect her at all? He believed so. He had faith in it.

But wasn't faith just another word for hope?

He hoped that Isabel would come soon. He hoped it very much. It was after four o'clock. School must have ended by now, he thought. A day and a half had passed, but Isabel hadn't returned. And still didn't come . . . At least Nina was at his side. She seemed to like the young woman. Even more: she appeared to have formed an intense trust in her. The dog was a comfort. Perhaps the last one he had left. She was big and strong and had a protective instinct. But would she be able to take on what might be lurking out there? And would he be able to? He thought of the night before last when Isabel and the young woman had knocked on the door of his workshop. He had noticed the glimmer of light coming through the crack in the door.

Sometimes, when he looked at the young woman who called herself Martha, he had the strange feeling that her whole body was steeped in the color of that light. It could also be seen in her eyes from time to time.

He wondered what she reminded him of. Then he remembered his visit many years ago to a copper foundry. Yes, that had been a very similar sort of color. Warm, intense, mysterious.

The young woman was asleep. She slept almost all the time.

And she hardly ever seemed to want to eat anything.

Christian Albert tried to distract himself. Tried to think about how Martha could be made as comfortable as possible in his cottage.

He didn't want to leave her alone. He didn't know what would happen if he went out into the open. But it was still daytime, rays of sunlight breaking through the cloud cover. Some of the treetops seemed dusted with gold. The dangerous darkness was still far away. So he dared.

He took an almost empty jam jar from the shelf, washed it out, put on his coat, and left the cottage. Nina stayed with the young woman.

Christian Albert wanted to collect fir and spruce needles in the forest. He was going to put them in the warm water later when Martha took the bath he had suggested to her. He hoped that the needles would give the weak woman some strength. After all, the needles with their wax-covered skin defied all the hardships of the seasons. There was an old freestanding bathtub in the cottage at the end of the kitchenette. Two mirrors cleverly placed in the corners caught daylight for it.

As he set out, Christian Albert thought of his childhood and how his father had taken him on forays through the forest.

In his memory his father had the face of lush fruit. A face that always had a radiance about it—even where the shadows of the trees deepened. His father had always raved about nature, had shown him the dead wood in the forest and how it made room for new life. Before Albert, his only child, his father had fought at the front in World War II. It was only years later that Christian Albert learned what a fervent Nazi he had been.

Later? A dangerous word. A useful trick of memory.

No, not later. He had already known, as a boy. It hadn't taken much to figure it out. Not much, no.

But the boy had never bothered his father with questions. He had always been eager to hear the story of how nature was indomitable and created space for itself everywhere. He had not wanted to know anything about how death created space for itself.

When a person was lost, some Black Forest people liked to tell a legend. The old legend of the stray weed that grew in some places in the forest. Whoever stepped on it would lose their way hopelessly. But it was not the witchweed's fault that Christian Albert did not return.

Martha von Falkenstein would not get to enjoy a bath of fir and spruce needles that evening.

8

The first hours of school that morning after her mysterious encounter with the woman were held without Isabel.

Usually a day off school was Isabel's greatest joy. But this time, she could not rejoice.

At dawn on the first of November—when the fog had lain like a rolling sea between the hills—the group home's counselor had driven her on her rickety motorcycle from Hofsgrund to a doctor in Günterstal. The doctor had renewed the bandage that the counselor had put on her the night before when she had noticed the bite wound on Isabel's hand.

The doctor gave her a shot that had hurt like hell.

The night of the incident in the woods, Isabel had returned very late to what was officially known as the "Residential Group Home for the Socialization of Troubled Youth." A stupidly stilted name, Isabel had always thought.

Isabel had expected the counselor to freak out. But she hadn't. She had been composed and had simply seemed worried. That was all. She said she had tried to reach Isabel four times on her cell phone. No signal. She had waited for Isabel to return, even though she had that evening off. Everyone in the home knew that the counselor always left early to bang her new boyfriend. She always acted well-mannered, but in truth, she was not a bit different from the five teenagers she cared for.

And at twenty-three, she wasn't that much older.

Isabel had claimed that the bite wound had come from a stray dog.

Why bother telling what had happened to her in the forest? No one would have believed such a story. Once you were a suspect youth, it could happen quickly: without any recourse, one was accused of being psychotic or something. No thanks, not a good idea. Isabel knew all about it. Knew it very well.

The counselor seemed to believe the story of the stray dog. And after the doctor and she had been satisfied, she had driven Isabel to school for fourth period.

Isabel's class report had been a disaster. Isabel hadn't had a good feeling about it for weeks, ever since it had been revealed who she would be giving it with. The random draw had teamed her up with a classmate she didn't like. A sickly sweet asshole.

That classmate, who was used to basking in guys' gazes and easy A's, had been horrified when the feedback on their report *Are Human Lives Predetermined?* had turned out to be pretty much a foregone conclusion. They had gotten a flat-out F on it.

Each two-person team had received one joint grade. The F had definitely been the worst grade that girl had ever gotten. Afterward, she had lost her shit, of course, and had blamed Isabel for everything. Which was not that far off the mark, of course.

But Isabel didn't care. She had even enjoyed the meltdown a little bit. But only briefly. Then she had again felt what she had felt that whole day: how hard it was for her to face the day. Again and again in her mind's eye she saw the charred creature that had emerged from the well that night. The young woman. Her mind searched for answers as if caught in the impassable realms of a dream.

∽

Isabel's school, Bartholomae Herder High School, was a mile and a half from Hofsgrund, in the next town over. When she returned to her shared rooms after class, she was alone. She wanted to be by herself.

Usually, she rode her bike. But now, she wanted to walk. Isabel enjoyed the cool air. Enjoyed the autumn sky, which was white and void. Bare delicate tree branches poked into the white. She passed the stone fountain in the center of town, where she often lingered on muggy summer days to refresh herself with its clear water. That's when the images surfaced again—the image of the crumbling well deep in the forest next to the chapel. The image of the black creature. She tried to blot it out of her mind.

This was not that place. It was beautiful. She looked at the edge of the fountain and the moss that grew through its brittle perimeter. Even though it was autumn, the crystal-clear stream descended onto the jagged stones just as it did on sun-drenched days.

An old woman leaned over the fountain, washing out a piece of laundry. Isabel wanted to smile at the woman, but then Isabel noticed that she had glassy, unworldly eyes and menacing air. Despite the cool weather, she was scantily clad. The dress she was wearing—a nightgown?—was tattered. One could see her breasts hanging low. The skin sagged wrinkled from her scrawny arms. Isabel made to hurry back on her way, but the old woman suddenly began to speak as she continued washing.

"I'm washing the linen from the past few days. It won't get clean, no." When Isabel did not respond to the words, the woman kept on talking without a glance at her.

"His name was Paul, the young man. Went to your school. And there was another young woman, went to your school. I know where they disappeared to, too." Now the old woman looked up and fixed her cool gaze on Isabel. "I also know who will disappear next."

Isabel hurried on, but she couldn't resist turning back to look at the woman. Then she saw it. Saw that a deep red was seeping from the piece of laundry into the water of the fountain. A red that looked like blood.

That afternoon, Isabel did not set out—as she had promised—to see Christian Albert and the stranger he was harboring. She couldn't. She didn't feel up to it. Maybe she would make it the next day when her regular visit to the old man was scheduled anyway.

Zoe, a roommate whose beauty, dark-skinned and impeccable, Isabel envied, had pot. They smoked it on the balcony, in the cool air. Gloomy Fynn, the only one in the group home she couldn't stand, wasn't there, thank god. Voices drifted up from downstairs. On the house's ground floor was an old restaurant, and smells of heavy, delicious food constantly drifted up.

The inn had existed when Hofsgrund had made the headlines early during the Third Reich. An English school class had been caught in a sudden snowstorm during their hiking vacation. The tragedy had claimed several lives. In the media, Nazi propaganda had hailed the small-town citizens who had "relentlessly" tried to save the English children. All sorts of old articles about it hung on the walls in the inn's parlor. It was as if the somber-faced innkeeper longingly and a little enviously dreamt of those "good old days."

Isabel enjoyed feeling the weed take hold of her senses. Another roommate, who had MS and was in a wheelchair, joined them. The pot, he told them, reduced the annoying twitching of his legs.

⌇

The next day, Isabel again failed to visit Christian Albert at his cottage. Since he did not have a telephone, she couldn't apologize to him.

That day she got stomach cramps at school. After her third class, she went to the secretary's office and had herself released to go home.

She spent most of the rest of the afternoon and evening in her room watching episodes of some old series, not something she did often.

Only once did she make a brief appearance in the kitchen, blinking with a pale face at the blackboard on which the individual daily appointments of the residents were noted. She looked with ponderous eyes at the photo of Greta Thunberg that the counselor had hung on the wall—surely to show them again what a single person could achieve. That it was possible to shape a better world. But in almost all cases, Isabel thought, the past was too dark to fight against. Too dark for the future, stronger than it was. She took a yogurt from the refrigerator that had been expired for a few days. When she finished it, she slipped onto the balcony to have a smoke. And to wrap herself in the fine bluish haze that matched the one in her head.

The young man she always met at the farm came to her mind. She felt a need to speak to him. Not knowing what she would sayto him. Not knowing how he could help her.

Later, her housemates would say that Isabel had seemed absentminded that evening, absorbed. They stated that this happened often, though, and that they had not thought anything of it.

What they could not report was the dream that haunted Isabel that night. She dreamt of the chapel in the forest in the dark. She saw the naked stranger in front of her, who had crawled out of the ruined well and then transformed into a pretty young woman with curls and bare pale skin. In the dream, her pale skin shimmered in the darkness. Iasbel heard the woman's voice: *Come to me!* Isabel tried to reach her. The road seemed endless. When she arrived, the mysterious stranger was no longer there.

Instead, she saw a face. A face she knew and had missed for so long. Her mother's.

"Don't be afraid!" her mother said. "Help the young woman!" There was a great urgency in her voice.

No, no one knew about that, later. However, there was a lot of talk and conjecture. Later. When nothing could be done.

꙳

Tristan stood in the darkness. He looked at the wooden structures in front of him, in the middle of the forest: a rather small house and, next to it, a second one that was even smaller. He smiled at the thought of how vulnerable these tiny houses were. How lost. Just as lost as Martha.

He had found her, finally. Had sensed her nearness all along but had not been able to locate her. Yet with each drop of life he had tasted, his senses had become more alert. They had led him here. At first, he had sensed a force that would not let him get any closer to these two houses. Something was working there. Something was holding him back. He knew the force. It lived in his memory. A hint of light that reached him from the past. But now, there was nothing to hold him back.

Martha would not be safe until she had survived the first eight days. Temporarily safe. He knew his mission. The unalterable trajectory on which they were both headed, toward their destiny. After exactly eight days, he would no longer be able to kill her. Until the chosen ones were selected and faced each other in the deciding battle.

But the end of the eight days was still a long way off. He knew she was still weak. So weak. He would have an easy time of it. The outcome would be final before she could even get to her feet.

The old man had also made it easy for him. Putting an end to his existence had been as easy as eating roasted beaver meat. He had liked roasted beaver meat. Back then, in the days that now lay deep beneath the sedimentary rock.

Suddenly, Tristan noticed a teenage girl approaching the two small cottages. He felt her heartbeat. Smelled the sweat from her body's pores and her fear. Navigating this new time proved to be no challenge. It was as if he could effortlessly draw on the knowledge of a foreign language. He clearly perceived what was going on in people's minds. And what he discovered pleased him. Even if the sounds and noises were different, he sensed how effective it still was: the voice of violence.

The voice of violence.

He could have heeded it again. The young woman who was now pounding on the door of the larger house was at his mercy. But he wanted to take his time. No need to rush. He wanted to enjoy it.

He thought of his sword, Xanas, and that it would soon find its way back to him. He remembered the joy he felt holding it in his hands. How it felt when his fingers closed around the hilt.

He often let the blade slide gently across his palm to feel its curve and sharpness. Some nights he pressed the sheathed sword against him. He remembered exactly how the wood of the scabbard had smelled and how it had reminded him of his childhood. Of his training in the use of such a weapon in the outer courtyard of the castle, when he had been a squire to his master, the Count of Staufen. Xanas was light, flexible, and possessed a balance that gave a gentle forward thrust. In battle, the sword vibrated in a barely noticeable way, like a tuning fork.

For now, he held hands the sword he had picked up at the fishing and weapons store. It was made of sturdy, suitable material and had a good length. However, it was heavy in hand. When it met solid resistance, the handle began to tremble. The center of gravity of the sword was much too far from the guard.

But he accepted these weaknesses without grudge. He had resharpened both sides of the blade with damp flat pebble sandstones, as he had sometimes done as a boy. The sword had already proven what deeds it was capable of. It would serve its function now, too.

Martha was weak. Much too weak. She was lost. Unable to gather strength to face him. Soon he would possess her sword as well. Reuniting what belonged together. Aurin and Xanas. Both blades were needed to seal the end.

At this thought, he smiled again, but all at once, he felt it return, the tinge of light that came to him from a distant time. It brought back to him the hot night wind brushing the deck of the two-masted ship, which had docked at a hidden cove. He thought of the two of them lying side by side in the belly of the ship, the night before the siege of Damiette began. How he and the warrior who had fought fearlessly by his side had suddenly become just a woman and a man again. How her hair had fallen, how she had bared her chest to him, how her lips had parted. A longing came over him, and the cruel sensation of guilt. But he would resist that feeling. She had broken the oath. It was not he who was the traitor, but she. He would push back the light. He, Tristan Nightsworn, would show no mercy.

IO

Can you hear me? I am speaking into the
darkness.
It is hard to speak into the darkness.
It's hard to speak when you're waiting for an
answer in vain.
Mama, will I be with you?

S he sounded close, the voice in the dream that had
spoken to Isabel and told her to seek the woman. As
close as it had ever been. *I should have guessed it then,* she
thought.

❧

Isabel climbed out of the window and ran into the forest
at night—all the way to the cottage. Through the tangle of
black branches and the velvety blue haze, she saw the stars
shimmer.

There was no light there. Neither in the workshop nor
in the house. Isabel could hear Nina barking inside even
before Isabel could pound on the door. No one opened for
a long time. She blew warmth into her hands. She looked
around in all directions. The blackness exhausted her eyes.
But she got the feeling that there was something out there.

Behind her, between dense rows of trees. Something that watched her steadily.

She even thought she saw something gleaming blue, not far away.

The door opened, and the dog jumped toward Isabel. Her front paws landed below her throat. Isabel tumbled backward to the ground. The dog's face was above her.

She heard a growl. Drool dripped down on her.

She had never seen Nina so angry. She had obviously expected an attacker. When Nina realized who she had brought down, she let go of Isabel. But she kept on barking at the night, a bark that echoed between the trees.

Isabel was still lying on the cold, hard earth when she saw the woman standing in the doorway. The woman who had crawled out of the well's maw two nights before. The woman made a gesture, and Nina came to her and trotted back into the house. She helped Isabel up and hastily closed the door behind them. She locked the door.

"Thank god you're here," she said. The stranger's voice sounded lonely and lost, like a voice groping its way through unfamiliar rooms.

❧

Martha von Falkenstein told her about Christian Albert's disappearance and said, "I tried. I tried to see what happened to him, but I failed. Fear clouded my vision."

Isabel didn't know what that meant: *I tried to see.* She asked, but Martha did not answer. *She sees me,* Isabel thought. *Sees me very clearly. She can see into the last dark corner, where my dreams are.*

Then Martha suddenly spoke of a task that Isabel must fulfill before something terrible happened. Because she was too weak to do it.

The thoughts twisted and turned in Isabel's head. She was overcome by the dreadful feeling that the stranger herself could be responsible for the old man's disappearance. But something inside her told her that it was not so—an inner voice of some sort.

Why did you deliver me to this fate, Mama? So that I could be with you?

Martha pressed something into her hand. When Isabel's fingers opened, she saw a lock of Martha's hair, tied with a delicate green fiber, lying on her palm. Stinging nettle, she guessed. She knew these fibers from her childhood. She saw her mother's hands in front of her. Saw how she had shown her how to tie flowers with them.

There was a leather bag in Isabel's hand, too, containing pieces of charcoal. Underneath the charcoal were two stones, with delicate ornaments on the outside that shone through with a reddish hue.

"Bloodstones," Martha von Falkenstein explained. "Specular iron. Hematite. Rocks that were once mined from the cliffs in this area."

"What do you want me to do?" asked Isabel.

"You need only start walking, and your feet will carry you along the twists and turns of the forest to a clearing where once there was a charcoal pile, in a time so distant that it is almost no longer true. But only almost. If you rub the two bloodstones together in this clearing, they will quickly strike sparks. With them, you light the charcoal, and you put the lock of hair into the flames. You will see a reflection, your own. And then it will appear. At least . . . that's what I hope."

"What will appear?" Isabel asked.

"The sword."

Suddenly, Nina lowered her big head. The fur on her neck and between her shoulder blades bristled. Her dark lips drew back, revealing two rows of pointed teeth. Nina's gaze was fixed on the bolted door. She let out a growl. Then she began to bark, dark, hoarse, threatening. She approached the door. Once, twice. And then she stopped barking and uttered something that sounded like a whimper.

A dull thud rang out as something heavy banged against the cabin's door, moved away, and struck it again. The door shook in its frame. A cool breeze invaded the room through a crack at the top. A voice could be heard from outside.

"Found you at last." The voice pierced through the door. "Finally. It took me a little while. Too long for my taste." Again, a heavy thud against the timber.

"A good shelter," called the voice. "Has a special feel of . . . love. Didn't make it easy for me to pay you a little visit. It even—how shall we say—shut me out. But violence helps. Especially against the sickness of love. You know what I'm talking about, don't you?" Again, whoever was out there struck the door with incredible force. It could hardly withstand the blow. The door bent inward and barely hung on its hinges. Behind it, a man was now visible, with menacing, pitiless eyes, and the blade of a sword with which he lashed out, splintering wood. Inevitably, he made his way inside to the two women. His physical form briefly dissolved before Isabel's eyes, and she felt she was looking at a beast that was about to tear her apart.

The door cracked, groaned, gave way.

Martha took staggering steps toward a garden rake leaning gainst the wall in a corner and grabbed it. But she was so weak she was barely able to lift it.

Isabel wanted to help her but could not. Her limbs were frozen. Only her eyes moved and saw the terrible thing that happened next.

The man squeezed his way in toward them. With him, a gust of wind swept leaves through the opening. He was wearing a cloak made of a material she didn't know, yet it made her shiver. Without giving Isabel a glance, he moved toward the cornered Martha. He let the sword circle slowly in his hand twice like a flashing wheel of death.

"You've looked better," he said to her as if they were old acquaintances. "But that was long ago. You know memories can be deceiving." He struck out, the blade slicing through the air. Isabel thought she heard the sound before it happened, the sound of blood splattering. She heard a yelp from Nina. The dog lunged at the attacker. And then the sound did come.

The man had severed Nina's right ear with a sword stroke. But Nina, bravely, did not give up. She lunged at the man, bit, jumped back. She fought. Fought the hopeless fight.

Isabel felt the numbness dissolve and life return to her body. She grabbed Martha by the arm and pulled her along toward the hatch in the floor where the pantry was. Isabel knew that there was a secret passage down there that led out into the open. Christian Albert had once very proudly shown it to her. She pulled the hatch open. They hastily dropped through, and Isabel tried to lock the door in the darkness. Her fingers trembled, and it took an excruciatingly long time before she managed it. The two of them rushed down the narrow staircase. Above her, Isabel heard the man rattling the door. Heard his angry voice. A blow from the sword burst the wood.

◦

The two of them crawled laboriously through a short underground tunnel and escaped out into the night. Martha collapsed to the ground, exhausted. Isabel helped her up.

"Who is that man?" she wanted to know.

Martha did not look at her. Her gaze was lost in the distance as she said, "I'm afraid he's more than just a man. He's a monster who knows how to kill."

"What do you mean?"

"He's a servant of sorts."

"Servant? Of whom?"

"A servant of doom."

Isabel did not understand these words. She hoped to learn more. But Martha urged Isabel to leave her.

"Don't forget your task! It is important. It's not just we who are in danger."

It seemed that any resistance was futile. Isabel reached into her coat pocket. For a moment, she feared she had forgotten the items Martha had handed her in the cabin. But they were still there.

"Go now, run!" Martha called out, as Isabel disappeared between the dark tree trunks.

II

Martha only managed to stay on her feet for a short time. Then she slumped back onto the cold earth. Night pressed on her eyelids, and she felt the need to close her eyes. No more visions to pierce her—no glimmering either of hope or of fear.

She longed to return to the vastness from which she had come.

But then she thought of Nina, the dog. Of how fearless she had been. How she had fought.

Every spark of life, no matter how small, was at risk. They had to be defended. This thought made her realize her responsibility, and it strengthened her courage. She, of all people, would have to fight.

She would face this fight. She would not give up. Never.

Dragging her legs stiffly behind her, Martha crawled forward on her elbows. At last, she managed to sit up. Like a sudden gust of wind, she once again felt the nearness of her nemesis. She was sure: Tristan Nightsworn had left the cabin and was after her. If she did not regain her strength quickly, the end was near. The end. She crept between the tree trunks, having to pause again and again to avoid falling. She felt him coming closer, but her senses seemed numbed by darkness. She scattered arnica root blossoms in front of her. They were delicate. Strawlike. Yellow. She had picked them here in the Black Forest eight hundred years ago, shortly before she had left her home and gone to war with a sword. These blossoms, which she had brought back from her dreams, now formed a protective shield for her.

When Tristan appeared in his chilling cloak not far from her, his senses could no longer find their way to her. He could no longer perceive her. He was only a few steps away from her. Martha did not move. She saw the gleaming blade. Steel, without a soul and yet imbued with a will. The will of a man who was focused on one single goal.

For a second time, she saw what she had noticed when he had broken into the cottage. It was not Xanas that he held in his hands. It was a different sword. But Xanas, she guessed, would not be long in coming.

She remembered Xanas well. A powder merchant from the traveling people had managed to reach into far eastern lands with his cart pulled by dogs—ancestors of Rottweilers. From his long journey, he had brought special tidings back to the Black Forest, news of the Japanese Katana sword. Tristan was taken with these stories. And so, the weapon he commissioned became a combination of a Japanese samurai sword and a saber. The heathens should—his intention was—feel death from their own blade. Xanas had a slightly slanted tip and a downward curved saber hilt that arched in the opposite direction of the edge. It lacked any kind of guard or thrusting blade. For a long time, this sword had been a symbol to Martha. For an emotion of which nothing had remained. She shivered at the thought of Xanas—named after a sunken black fortress in the woods. The fate of Tristan Nightsworn's family had supposedly been linked to it for generations.

Martha and her adversary faced each other among the towering trees. Tristan's eyes searched for her but did not detect her. The blade moved before him, searching. But it found nowhere to aim.

She listened for him. Heard his snort of rage. Then he seemed to notice something in the distance. All at once, he took off. She knew exactly what had caused his sudden agitation. She knew exactly where he was going. But there was nothing she could do to stop him.

12

Isabel had started to run. She felt like a path was unfolding beneath her steps—a path through the all-encompassing blackness.

She had no idea whether branches were tugging at her clothes, whether the path was ascending or descending, whether it led over roots or through thorny bushes. Nor was she aware of how long she had been moving. When she reached a clearing, she felt that this was the right place. A feeling overcame her that it was not she who had set out to find it, but that the place itself had come to her.

She squatted down and rubbed the stones together, lit the fire. Put Martha's strand of hair into it. The flames whispered under the star-embroidered arch of the sky, and sometimes a piece of charcoal consumed by the fire sank deeper into the embers like golden tinsel. As she gazed into the fire, she tasted the strange elongated plant on her tongue that she had eaten a few months earlier during her self-imposed time out in the forest.

With it came the stomach cramps that so often afflicted her—more intense than ever before.

Isabel fought the pain. She felt the importance of not giving up. Felt a responsibility that she couldn't pin to anything. It frightened her, and yet she could not escape. She complied with the order. She did everything Martha had told her to do. Almost everything.

Before the stranger had forced his way into the cabin, Martha had given her another gift: dried arnica blossoms, which, she claimed, could have a special effect. Isabel was to scatter them on her way to the clearing as a protective shield. To be invisible. But she had forgotten to scatter the yellow blossoms.

She stared into the fire, waiting for something to happen. But nothing happened. No reflection appeared, nor did a sword appear in the flames. Instead, another sword approached. She sensed it too late. She felt it as the shimmering bluish light fell across her back. She knew immediately whose blade it was.

"Did you find what you were looking for?" said the man who had entered Christian Albert's cabin. Like a stalking animal, he drew closer and closer.

"Yes, I did," she said offhandedly, without turning around, amazed at her own boldness.

"Where is it?" the voice hissed. It suddenly no longer sounded soft and ingratiating. Instead, it sounded like the voice of the night itself.

"Where have you hidden Aurin?"

A strange calm came over her for a few moments as she sensed the man was almost upon her. The throbbing in her temples eased. The peace of certainty surged through to her.

Mama, do you hear me? I am speaking into the darkness.
It's hard to speak into the darkness.

Drops of blood ran down from the man's blade and dripped onto her hair. Then came the panic.

Isabel rushed away. She ran faster than she had ever run before in her life. But it was useless.

13

Martha groped her way forward. A wind rose and moaned in the darkened air. She was barely able to hold herself upright on her limp limbs. She felt her hunger taking hold of her whole being. The scent of an animal reached her, and she tried to follow it. She knew that this animal was significant. It could help her. She needed a special drink, one that would give drive and give her strength, so that she would be ready. A potion that would finally unleash the life in her and lead her back to her old strength. But she was too weak to locate the animal precisely. She followed the faint trail, running in a southerly direction. Followed the up-and-down path between the trees. Sometimes her knees gave way. She fell and cut her skin on a sharp-edged stone. Again and again, the path slipped away from her. She found herself lying among brush and nettles gazing up at the flickering starry dots of Orion far above her.

Suddenly she heard a small voice singing. A little song warbled through the air: *Tea for two . . .*

In a mysterious glow, a boy approached, still singing his song. When he was only a few steps away, she saw that he was wearing a ragged short-sleeved shirt and shorts and faded socks, and that his shoes were barely holding together. She saw his thin bare legs. She saw that he had blue lips marked by cold. His face looked white and waxy. In his right hand, he held a small, withered orange.

She stood up. The boy stopped singing. His eyes rested forlornly on her.

"Who are you?" she asked.

"I'm almost like you," he replied. "Almost like you. I've come back. I don't belong here. But I've been back here longer than you. I've been wandering. I sing the song. It calms me. It calmed me even back then when the snow came. But it didn't do me any good."

"Back then?" asked Martha.

"I'm almost like you," he repeated. "I don't belong here. I come from England. I'm a student at the Strand School in London-Brixton. I am twelve years old. But that's not now. Not now, no. Back then. I persuaded my father to let me come along. Ten days of Easter vacation in the Black Forest. A hike with our German teacher. That was the goal. But in the end, in the end we found another destination. The teacher didn't listen to anyone. Not to the landlady who warned of the sudden onset of winter. Not to the woodcutters along our path. 'Keep going!' he kept shouting. Though he didn't know the area. But the winter, which was only sleeping and not yet driven away, did not care what our teacher said. There were twenty-seven of us when we started marching. Five did not return. I am one of the ones who did not return. But I kept the provisions, our provisions, which each of us was allowed to take with us—an orange. The blizzard couldn't take it away from me. Not the snow, and not even death . . . I am twelve years old. I am not cold anymore. I'm on the move. I am almost like you."

A strange silence settled in. The boy threw the orange into the air above him like a juggling ball and caught it again. The two looked at each other, two souls lost to the night. Martha wanted to say something, but there were no words in her.

"You need help," the boy said. "I know what to do. Come!" Humming his little song, the boy led the way, and Martha followed him as fast as she could along the path, which was a frayed ribbon leading in twists and turns through the darkness.

The path rose steadily, and they reached the northern head of Kyb Rock, where the sparse remains of a castle lay, grudgingly revealed by the forest.

The boy smiled at Martha, waved briefly once more, and disappeared among the remains of the wall. He took his little song with him. Martha watched him go, saw him toss the orange high into the air two more times. Then he was gone.

She turned, walked a few steps ahead, and spotted the traces of an overgrown, mossy stump of tower. Suddenly she sensed the presence of two creatures, barely visible in the darkness, but directly in front of her: a red deer cow and her calf, crouched between the hind legs of its mother, suckling for milk. The calf was a male and already quite large, certainly over six months old. Its white juvenile spots appeared to have already disappeared. The two animals did not register Martha's presence at first, but then the calf suddenly pushed itself flat on the ground. Martha felt it stop breathing, how it reflexively closed all body orifices so that it was almost odorless. Only the beating of its heart testified to its presence. The mother looked in their direction and stamped several times threateningly with its front legs on the ground. Then the two seemed to sense that there was no danger from Martha. The stomping ceased. The calf rose. The two did not run away. They remained calmly in place.

Instinctively, Martha lowered herself to the ground and crawled slowly toward the doe. When she was under her, her lips approached the teats of the animal, opened. She drank the milk. She felt the taste in her mouth, the taste of the wild, and how the milk sank down her throat. She felt her body strengthening more and more. Greedier and greedier, she drank until the taste of blood mingled with the milk, and the doe finally jumped back and took off, followed by her fawn.

But it didn't matter. Martha had drawn strength. Martha von Falkenstein's life, her new life, had now finally begun. And she would know how to use it.

14

Enclosed by towering trees, Lake Flint lay beneath the scattered silver of the Milky Way. The rowboat carrying the two brothers rocked on the expanse of water.

Their headlamps suggested the temperaments of the two. One beam was a gentle stream into the night; the second was like a searchlight that wouldn't come to rest.

"Is it that time already?" asked Balder, who had only recently turned fifteen. "Should we go see?"

"You have to be patient," said Daniel, who was a year and a half older. "It doesn't happen that fast."

"But maybe it will."

But maybe it will—that was Balder's favorite phrase. He threw it at all the impossibilities of life. The other four brothers and especially his father were annoyed by it. Again and again they said that he had difficulty in correctly comprehending context, understanding limits. *He just doesn't get it,* they said. And: *What can you do about it?* Daniel knew that Balder's powers of comprehension often let him down. Instead, he seemed to have a flair for certain other, unnamed things. When they were little, their father had skinned Daniel's favorite rabbit alive—and he had done it while his son watched, specially summoned for the purpose. To make it clear that Daniel was not to form an emotional attachment to the rabbits kept on the farm. He remembered how their father had held out the naked, dripping piece of meat to him that had once been the beloved animal. Then their father had left Daniel alone.

Daniel remembered the silence that overcame him. The silence in which tears were stifled. In that silence, Balder had suddenly appeared. He had made long ears with his hands and had hopped around, as if it were the natural thing to do. That a little boy could fill the gap left by a rabbit. Daniel had flown into a rage and had lunged at his brother. Had punched him in the face until blood had spurted from Balder's nose, bright red in the afternoon heat that weighed heavily on the farm.

But then Daniel had understood. Had understood that this spectacle was probably Balder's only way of giving him comfort. And it was the only consolation given to him on that childhood day that united heat and death.

Much more often, however, it was the other way around. It was Balder who, seemingly for no apparent reason, attacked Daniel and beat him. Sometimes the youngest brother took on all the other brothers at once, and it was extremely difficult to hold him back. For some unknown reason, he would suddenly become furious. Even the color of his eyes seemed to change. It became bright, even iridescent.

"I want to swim," Balder said all of a sudden.

"Already forgot why we're here?" asked Daniel, pointing to the fishing rod in his brother's hands.

Daniel hadn't intended to take Balder with him. He enjoyed escaping the cacophony of family voices whenever possible. Balder had begged to be included. *Get lost!* was the answer he'd gotten. But it was no use. When Daniel set off with his rod and the other fishing gear, his brother had followed behind him, across the field that lay in the evening light. Daniel was sure there would be trouble. His mother always worried about where Balder was. And his father argued with her about it. Because he didn't like people you had to keep a careful eye on. Maybe that's why, Daniel thought, when the family sat around the table at dinner, he never looked any of the boys in the face. He looked off into nowhere—as if it were a more comfortable place than the kitchen. But perhaps there were other reasons. Sometimes their father would say, "You children have been twisted away from me by your mother." There was no question about that, Daniel thought. Considering the way he would go at their mother. How the whites of his eyes widened, as if the world could burn away in them.

Daniel switched off his headlamp and looked at the darkness of the lake. He tried to get his mind off things. He tried to think again about the strange girl who occasionally came to the old Black Forest farm where Daniel lived with his brothers, mother, and father. Schleiermoos Farm, nearly four hundred years old, had been in the family for generations. It sat above Hofsgrund. She sometimes came cycling up the hill to buy eggs. The girl who seemed so brooding but occasionally flashed a smile he couldn't forget. A smile that stayed with him. He hadn't realized how powerful a smile could be. A simple smile that showed a small crooked tooth. Sometimes he saw her in a dream and secretly touched himself.

Daniel knew that the girl did not live with her parents but in a shared home for teenagers with mental issues. Another girl from there, Zoe, was in his class. But the girl who smiled so beautifully was not. She was in the other home-room. He had found out her name: Isabel. It had been a few months since she had suddenly, briefly disappeared.

After two days the residents of the surrounding area had gone in search of her—they feared that something ter-rible had happened. Daniel remembered it well. Remem-bered the search parties that had been formed. The husky voices of mothers, all trying to give directions, and the silent, closed faces of fathers. Above all, he remembered hope. The hope that it would be him who found Isabel.

The search operation turned out to be pointless. She had simply run off into the woods, people decided, long-ing for a green to grow over the asphalt of her life and a sky framed by leaves. Daniel wasn't the one who'd found her. It was other people, who didn't care about her smile or why she would want to escape into the green. Presumably, Isabel had had to give a series of explanations, and they had shut her away. In any case, it had taken quite a while for her to show up at school again.

Daniel got angry when he thought about these people. Mad at the dark night, mad at the green. At all the colors. Furious that he wasn't alone on the lake but had his broth-er in the boat with him. He also felt angry that they hadn't used the phosphorescent rubber lures that attracted the walleyes but had absolutely had to use worms just because Balder liked to hold their squirming little bodies between his fingers so much.

Daniel hadn't been able to deny him that, even though it reduced their chances of catching anything. You had to be damned lucky to catch a walleye with a worm, even in this part of the lake, where among the lily pads often turned out to be a good spot. But Daniel knew a ruse that just might work. He had told Balder to spear a worm on a tiny mormyshka, the hook with a long shank ending in a perforated lead drop. When the sun was gone, the walleye would come up from their cold murky depths almost to the surface to hunt. Such a tiny wagging lure could be tempting to them. But whether they could sense it well enough, Daniel didn't know. The worm left only a faint scent, intended for hunters with delicate noses like eels.

"Don't forget to crank," he said to his brother, showing him again how to put a tremor on the string with his wrist. Then he surrendered his eyes to the darkness again. A fish clicked in the water but was much too far away. After that, again, only the gurgling and smacking of tiny waves against the boat could be heard. How long had they been out? Daniel did not know. He was shivering. He felt lonely. He felt a kinship with the boat, bobbing along in a dark expanse. To Balder, he said, "When we catch one, we'll leave." He listened to the wind and how it slipped through the trees on the shore. He tried to imagine the life that the dark forest held. The animals making last forays before the air acquired its winter edge. He thought of the thirsty mosses. Of the vast stealthy army of mushrooms.

"What's that?" he suddenly heard his brother ask, leaning out of the boat. And then Daniel saw it. At first, the thought popped into his head that there must be a diver down there somewhere. But he had never known the secluded lake to be used by divers. That anyone would be diving here in the cold autumn night seemed unlikely to him. What Daniel saw could not have been caused by a flashlight or the like. No, it had to have another origin, this glow. A mysterious pale blue glow shimmered under the water's surface, creating space for itself there in the dark underwater world. It enveloped the small boat and the place where they had dropped the bait. He watched it for a few heartbeats. Then the glow disappeared, and there was nothing but the soft billowing black. As he still restlessly watched, he was left with a feeling that sometimes overcame him after sleep.

The feeling of a recurring dream that had vanished again without leaving a trace. Daniel exhaled in bursts. He hadn't realized he'd been holding his breath.

Something bit, and Balder, who could never hold back at such moments, began to reel in the line. Much too quickly, Daniel feared. But then he saw the struggling body of an eel being pulled out of the water by Balder. Probably without knowing it, his brother had done everything right. Eels had to be dealt with quickly. Otherwise, they would retreat with the swallowed bait to a nearby shelter, and the line would become entangled in it. It was—as Daniel quickly realized—a beautiful specimen. His trained eye estimated it at just under twenty-four inches, between two and three pounds. Balder received the animal with a joy rarely bestowed on creatures doomed to die. As his brother held the still writhing eel aloft, it seemed to Daniel that for a few moments, its body took on a shimmering light blue hue in the night air.

It really was time to get some sleep.

⌒

After they reached the shore again and moored the boat, Balder walked behind him through the forest night. Daniel heard the sloshing of water and how the bucket holding the eel rumbled against his brother's legs. Surely Balder would lie awake until morning, tossing and turning. "A good catch!" he kept shouting into the darkness. Daniel would have loved to be angry with him. Like their other brothers, who needed him as a target for their anger, would be. But he couldn't be mad. He thought of his mother and how glad she would be to see Balder return unharmed. And he thought of how she would gut and prepare the eel. She usually prepared herb pancakes to go with it, which were very tasty.

When she smoked it, she always put a sprig of pine in the oven embers, as she did with the hams that hung in the old hayloft under the roof. This provided a unique aroma. The spicy, resinous smell that rose from the flames, that was the scent of his mother.

But first, Daniel thought, they would keep the eel back in the discarded bathtub that was rusting outside the barn. And Balder could play with him.

It was getting chilly. The wind moved more strongly in the trees. Suddenly something shattered the silence. A scream that pierced through the forest. Someone was calling for help. A woman's voice, desperate, shrieking.

The two brothers stopped abruptly. Again and again, they heard the voice, which seemed to come closer and closer, even though their headlamps did not pick out a figure anywhere. But branches were cracking under heavy, quick footsteps that appeared to be following them, and the rustling of swirling leaves could be heard. Then Daniel heard a sound he had never heard before. The sound of a weapon slicing through the air. Like a long blade.

The woman's screams did not subside. In between came the low murmur of a man's voice: "Where is it? Tell me where it is!"

Daniel turned off his headlamp and instructed his brother to do the same. He told him not to make a sound. But Balder paid no attention. He said, "We have to be there, be there . . ." All at once, Balder ran off through dense brush into the impenetrable shadows of trees, toward a clearing from which the screams were now coming. Daniel ran after his brother. At the edge of the clearing, he caught up with Balder just in time to hold him back between dense bushes. Not twenty paces away, on the opening expanse, they saw the two figures, and behind them, the bare branches splayed into the dark sky.

Daniel saw that one figure was a man. A man who held something in his hands. A shiver came over him when he realized that it was a long sword, its blade gleaming pale in the starlight. The second figure had been dragged down to her knees. A young woman, from the silhouette. The brothers heard the man's piercing voice again, "Where is it?" She made no reply. Then, with a fine, barely perceptible sound, the blade drove through the air and sliced the young woman's head from her body. Daniel imagined he caught a dull sound as the head hit the ground. Balder dropped the bucket, the water rushed out in a gush, and with it, the eel wriggled into the grass. The man looked up and glanced in their direction. Seconds passed that seemed endless to Daniel, during which he didn't dare breathe. Then, finally, the man disappeared between the trees. Daniel still felt the throbbing in his temples as Balder ran through the bushes into the clearing. He seemed to have no sense of danger and to find the situation exciting. Daniel had to control him as quickly as possible before what had happened to the young woman happened to them. But his knees were so weak that he was barely able to follow his brother.

"There it is! There it is!" Balder had found the head, which was lying on the ground staring up with its eyes open. Daniel recognized the face. A face that had once worn a smile that had been his desire. A pretty smile that had shown a crooked tooth . . .

Shortly after, the two brothers also found the eel. Rather, they found what had once been an eel. What now lay there on the damp autumn soil was a sword. A strange-looking, oddly curved thing that somewhat resembled a saber and also a Japanese samurai sword. Balder fumbled for it and picked it up. When Daniel tried to hold him back, Balder snapped at his brother indignantly, "Don't touch me!" Daniel felt his brother's eyes brighten in anger. He sensed it, though he could barely make it out in the dark.

But only moments later, Balder let out a snicker. He swung the blade through the air. Then he held it horizontally in front of him, one hand on the hilt, the other supporting the blade. He could not take his eyes off the weapon. He even smelled it and seemed to want to absorb the scent of it deeply. Daniel felt as if his brother had been waiting a long time to find it.

15

When Martha von Falkenstein reached the clearing, brightness had already begun to mingle with the air. Mixed with the grass was blood.

She had come too late. Isabel's body lay lifeless in the grass, and where the head had been, she stared at a black gaping hole. She sensed that Tristan Nightsworn was still nearby but gradually moving away. His presence grew fainter and fainter. *Perhaps he has found what he was looking for,* she thought in horror. *Maybe we are already lost . . .* Then she registered something else. Close by—the presence of two young men. One of them exuded an enormous force that she could not name, but she feared that force. The other's flame of life was vulnerable. But there was something else in him. Something that inspired courage. Martha did not know exactly where the two men were at the moment. They certainly didn't seem to be far away. And she sensed it precisely. That their paths would soon cross.

She went on a harrowing search for Isabel's head. But she did not find it. So, finally, she returned to the body, got down on her knees, and said a prayer.

Despair came, and deep sorrow that Isabel had had to die. Tears streamed down Martha's cheeks at the thought of the sacrifice the young woman had made. Martha had not wanted her death. She had believed that she could prevent it. But she had failed.

She thought of the sweetness of life and what that life meant, held in the hollow of one's hand, to be thrown away, just like that. She was grateful to Isabel for all she had done.

All at once Martha flinched violently. Before her eyes, a tremor ran through the dead body, growing stronger and stronger until the steel tip of a blade pierced Isabel's ribcage from the inside. From the slashed corpse in a final gush of blood emreged a sword.

Aurin.

The sword that Martha had once wielded. Eight centuries ago. In a time so distant that it almost could not be true. As Martha looked down in horror at Isabel's mutilated corpse, from which Aurin had burst forth, she again cursed the mysterious, the merciless, the invisible forces that worked in this world and the next. Their strange courses. Their cruel excesses. And Martha cursed herself. She was painfully struck again by her guilt in Isabel's death. Influenced by dreams and vague premonitions, she had told the young woman what to do in an urgent effort to retrieve the sword. But she had not guessed that it could return only in this one horrible way.

She cursed the unfathomable task she bore. The sword disgusted Martha. She remembered how she had sworn centuries ago to never carry it again, to never fight with it again. But she knew now that she had no choice. As her hand closed around the hilt of the sword, the blood on the blade faded away. It was now shiny, radiating a dignity that would never suit its purpose.

Martha regarded the smooth, double-edged longsword. Her gaze traveled up the leaf-shaped blade, which tapered to a point. And then down the long gouge to the ends of the quillons, which were cut off at an angle and curved toward the blade. She studied the stylized pear-shaped pommel. And against her palm, she felt the pattern she had had engraved on the hilt. A pattern that seemed to swirl like a wind. The wind of change that seized all things—often with brute force—was what her mother had called Aurin. In all the stories she had told her two daughters, Martha and Keth, over and over again. In her sickly, coughing voice. The wind of time, the swirl of blood had brought the sword back to Martha.

The pear-shaped knob began to change, alter until it became an octagon with eight spokes. She knew that it had now begun, the age that was under the sign of the Eight. Eight fighters, one destiny. The destiny of all souls. Two of these fighters already existed. Tristan Nightsworn and herself. So there remained six. Six fighters who had to be found, who had to be chosen. Her adversary would not rest. He would try to get them all on his side.

Time was running out.

Martha rose in the gray light of morning as a gust of wind made the blades of grass in the clearing flash brightly. Behind her, mists stretched across the woodland through which she had wandered that night. Even though the sadness over Isabel's death had not yet left her, she sensed that something had changed. Martha's strength had returned. Her senses were now wide awake. She could trust them. They would take her far away when necessary and guide her back.

She left the horror of Isabel's mortal remains behind her. She had been lucky that Aurin had not fallen into the hands of her adversary. She held on to that thought as she set out, not knowing where it would lead her. The sword that had found its way to her was a high card. The decisive one? Somewhere out there was Xanas, the second sword. She could sense it.

One high card would not be enough. Not enough in the all-deciding battle that now lay ahead.

PART TWO

THE
CALL

16

*He feels it under his skin. He has not felt it in a
long time. He has often whispered the name to
no avail.*

Balder was afraid that he had done something wrong.
That he might have disappointed it, and perhaps it
had disappeared forever. He didn't want it to disappear.
He needed it. The creature that lived inside him.

He had known it since childhood.

It called itself Mistilo.

Perhaps the creature had only been in hiding.

There had been so much turmoil. So many people had
come to the farm. Had asked questions about the bodies
in the forest. Wanted to be told again and again what had
happened that night.

They asked about the old guy who was also dead.
Whether he and Daniel had seen anything.

The people had peered around with their tireless eyes.
That's when Mistilo had gone quiet. Mistilo was smart. It
didn't want to be found. Not yet. It lurked in the dark.

It would reveal itself one day. It would not be long now.
Balder sensed it.

Daniel would not left him alone. Had told him that
there was no way he could keep the sword. Had urged him.

Had wanted to get rid of the sword immediately. But it was beautiful. So beautiful.

Balder had let Daniel have his way. They had buried it together. At a place in the forest they knew well. Where no one ever strayed. There, as little boys, the six brothers had built a secret shelter out of branches and twigs.

Daniel seemed happy when the sword was buried.

He was suddenly no longer tense. Really relieved.

On the way back, Daniel had been cracking jokes.

He did not suspect at all. That Balder would dig up the sword again a short time later. When the hustle and bustle of the traditional ceremonial harvest slaughter started. When the butcher came and his father and brothers helped. Not a bit festive for the fattened pigs. When no one noticed that he was missing. That's when he had brought it back—the sword.

It could not be buried. It had to be alive, just like Mistilo.

A little later, there had been a funeral for the dead. The old guy was buried. He joined his wife in the grave. The mourners talked about how cruelly these people had died. They cried.

Balder didn't. Death, after all, feeds on the tears of the survivors. They should have known that! Besides, he didn't feel like crying. Because the sword had come back into his possession.

He thought of something. The right moment had been chosen. Nobody had seen it when he crept in the dining room to the shrine where a crucifix hung in the niche at the strongest supporting outer post of the house. Beneath Jesus, which already had a foot broken off, there was a shelf on which dusty figurines of saints and pictures were standing around. Beneath their feet lay the altar cloth, sort which poor Black Forest maids used to weave and carry from farm to farm as a minor source of income.

Balder took the altar cloth with him. Such a cloth was festive and appropriate for the sword, he thought. He wrapped it in it and hid it in the darkest of corner in the old hayloft of the farm. There it would wait. It would not have to wait long.

Saturday came. Everyone sat at the table and ate breakfast. His father drank Rossler liqueur made from Jerusalem artichokes. If the family was lucky, he drank only one. But that day, they were not lucky.

His father yelled at his brothers that they were doing everything wrong, lifting and hauling boxes around the farm. Were too slow. Didn't stack the crates properly. Were still damned useless fools on whom all his time and effort was wasted. Then his older brothers went with him to the market, the same as every Saturday.

Balder retreated to the hayloft under the roof. His eyes quickly adjusted to the sparse light up there. The hayloft was about ten yards wide, twenty yards long. Above was a room of similar size. But the floorboards were too precarious to stand on up there. He heard bugs up there and birds. An animal was scratching with its paws. Balder unwrapped the sword from the altar cloth. Held it in his arms like a beloved creature as he fell asleep lying on his back. He dreamed of blood and victory. When he awoke, he opened the old window that was so dirty it hardly let in any light. It was a sunny autumn day outside. The sun poured in, drawing triangles and squares on the floorboards, which were strewn with dust and leftover grain in between scattered feathers. A rat suddenly darted out from a dark corner. Balder stepped forward with lightning speed, the sword whirring through the air and putting an end to its life. Balder thought of his brothers and mother as he did. It was a pity that they would be dead, too. All of them.

When his older brothers returned from the market, their father yelled new insults at them. His tongue struggled with each word, was weakened from the liquor he had drunk on the way.

For dinner they ate shredded meat with mushroom cream sauce and kratzete, a thick, hearty pancake which their mother cut into pieces hot from the pan. As he ate, their father said grimly to Daniel, "Stop smacking your lips!" Daniel had been eating very quietly. But their father saw it differently: "Stop smacking, damn it!" He kicked the chair so hard that Daniel fell backward onto the floor. The back of his head hit the wooden floor hard. His mother was as his side in an instant.

"Get out of here," their father hissed. "Get out of here, all of you! Now! Only you stay!" He grabbed their mother's wrist.

༄

The attic was now in perfect blackness. But Balder's eyes had already become accustomed even to this blackness. Downstairs from the living area of the farmhouse, the pleading, the whimpering of his mother could be heard. Then he heard nothing more, but he still knew exactly what was happening. He saw before his eyes how his father pressed his mother's face against the bench of the tiled stove until she was almost unable to breathe. In winter the stove bench gave off a pleasant warmth. All year round, it stifled cries.

Suddenly Balder heard footsteps in the room above him. The rotten wood creaked. The footsteps moved slowly toward a place where the floor had broken apart and a large hole opened up. He stared up at the spot and saw a figure appear. It jumped down from the height, landed close to him, and went down on its knees. Then it rose and looked at Balder with piercing eyes. It was a man wearing a coat of intense, strikingly shimmering blue. Balder recognized the man from the night in the forest; it was he who had cut off the young woman's head. Balder remembered well. He did not feel fear, however. He felt awe. And a feeling like the joy of reunion.

"It's good to finally meet you," the stranger said. "And you found the sword for me. You are a talented young man. The others don't see it. But I see it well. I see very well what is hidden deep inside you. You no longer need to keep it hidden. You can bring it to life, just as you brought Xanas to life." Balder looked at the man. He felt the force of attraction emanating from him, the excitement his words evoked in him.

"You know it's time, my young friend, for your little secret to come forth," the man said with a half-sung sigh. It rose from a deep darkness such as Balder had never felt before, and which he recognized in a mysterious way. He knew that was where he would follow now.

He felt it under his skin. Yet, for a long time, he had not sensed it with him. He had often whispered the name to no avail.

Now it returned with indomitable strength. It was now finally ready to burst forth. The creature inside him. He had known its name since childhood. Everything that had been the Balder seemed to evaporate until nothing of him remained. Until only one name was left, floating in the darkness. Mistilo.

⌒

The man was still pummeling his cowering wife on the floor when a monstrous creature entered the rustic dining room. It stood on two legs but could not possibly be a human being. A clawed hand with sharp talons closed around the handle of a strangely curved sword. The man was so horrified by the sight that he hardly moved as the creature cut off his right arm and the blood poured over the wooden floor.

But the young man in the corner of the room had witnessed everything. He had tried in vain to help his mother but had been no match for his father's tremendous strength. He now held his breath as he witnessed what was happening to his father.

Daniel recognized his brother Balder in the terrible-looking creature.

Daniel followed the creature out into the cool air. The motion detector popped on, lights flooding the yard, and Daniel saw it leap over the large gate and race toward the fields. As fast as he could, Daniel followed the creature that had once been his brother. He almost fell over Marble, a farm cat that dashed for reassurance between his legs. Daniel kept running, and dark night enveloped him.

Then he lost sight of the creature. He wondered what to do. Turn back? He decided against it, although he instinctively sensed that he was in danger. That his life was threatened. But if there was even a slim chance of saving his brother, he had to take it. He began calling Balder's name, hoping he would hear that Daniel recognized him . . . and loved him.

Carefully, Daniel put one foot in front of the other, calling his brother's name over and over again. The farm was already a good distance behind him, but he thought he could hear their lead cow, Leonie, which he was so fond of. Only the other day, he had guided her back from the pastures to the barn together with the other cows and a basket full of potatoes—because they liked potatoes very much. Or maybe he just imagined hearing them mooing so he wouldn't feel so lost. He didn't know. Neither did he know where the creature had disappeared to. He followed his intuition, walking slowly down the slope where pastor pears hung ripe from the branches. When he reached the bottom, he was not far from the deep black strip where the dense forest began.

He got closer and closer to the forest. Felt the mighty presence of the towering spruces. Suddenly, he heard labored breathing in the meadow, just a few feet from the forest's edge. Then he discovered what lay there huddled on the cold earth. There was no monstrous creature there. It was his brother Balder, who was trembling all over. Lying on the ground next to him, Daniel saw the eerie sword they had found on the gruesome night of Isabel's murder. He had thought it was buried and gone forever. But he had been wrong. It had returned. And its diabolical blade had severed his father's arm with a barely perceptible swish.

But Daniel spared only a brief thought for the weapon. He was so glad to have found his brother. He didn't know what had happened to Balder, what the horrible transformation had been about. Only one thing mattered: he was alive. Balder looked up at Daniel as if searching for something.

For the very first time in his life, Daniel realized how important Balder was to him. That perhaps there was no one in the whole world as important to him as he was.

He made a move to help him up, but the hand he reached for was suddenly no longer a hand. Again, long, razor-sharp claws groped for him. Daniel quickly pulled back his hand. What rose up before him was the creature he had followed all this way to find his brother. He had lost Balder for good. He knew that now.

Daniel had never seen such a horrific creature before. It towered over him by at least two heads. It looked as if it had emerged from some swampy lowlands of fear. The large face with protruding teeth and the slavering longue leaned toward him. He felt the sharp claw touch his neck and heard a deep gurgling voice say, "Get out of here! Before I kill you!"

The clawed hand slowly withdrew from Daniel's neck. Behind the creature, he saw a silhouette and emerge from between the tall spruce trees. Daniel recognized him. It was the man in the long coat who had killed Isabel. The creature picked up the sword from the ground and slowly moved toward the man. It handed him the weapon in a submissive gesture.

Despite the darkness, Daniel thought he saw a smile on the man's face. Then the stranger turned and disappeared into the darkness of the forest. And the creature quickly followed him.

17

The streetcar made a discreet sound as it glided through the autumnal streets of Freiburg, as gentle as a melody. Such a tune could almost have made her forget the danger. The omnipresent danger. Almost.

Zoe didn't believe her own senses. She never had.

The instinct of danger, it was different. That's the one Zoe trusted.

Danger had a convincing voice. Zoe could hear it murmuring: *Come closer!*

﹏

Again she remembered yesterday's dream.

Of the dark, cool waters of Lake Flint, where she had sometimes swum as a child. Encircled by conifers, it stared up into the sky like an eye—a remnant from the distant past, when the earth was made of ice.

Come closer!

Again Zoe saw the figure before her, emerging from the water. The dripping hair, the piercing gaze. The finely curved lips in the gaunt face. And the bewitching voice— which spoke only two words: *Come closer!*

Was this dream connected with the recent horrible events? Zoe sensed it was, though she was not sure in what way. Four people murdered. That is to say, officially, there was talk of three killed: a student, Paul; a student, Isabel; and an old man named Christian Albert. There was still no trace of the young student teacher who had gone missing. But there was little doubt that she had also perished. Of Paul, who had been in Zoe's class, they had finally found one grisly piece, a cheekbone. Not to mention Isabel. She had been decapitated! All the media had reported on it, not just the regional ones. Did the man—the *being*—from her dream have something to do with it? Zoe tried hard not to face that question.

She thought about Isabel's funeral. Of the small Hofsgrund village cemetery on the hillside. She remembered the scattered leaves. As if to signal its approaching dominion, autumn had already pulled the colors out of them, making them brittle and fragile.

It had not seemed out of place to pursue such thoughts there. Where gravestones rose from the dark ground.

The cemetery had been thick with people.

Thick with eyes staring into the emptiness that death inflicted on them.

Most of the mourners had been young. Many classmates from Bartholomae Herder High School had come. Also, students from the surrounding areas. They had all come to pay their last respects to Isabel, who had died so cruelly.

Beheaded. Zoë's thoughts hissed that word tirelessly. She had been *beheaded*! As if in some grim past where daily life had consisted of such raw violence.

There had, of course, been no open coffin when she was laid out in the. It had been decorated with her favorite plant, ivy. And like that ivy, Zoe's thoughts entwined the casket during the funeral service. She wondered what a mortician did with a corpse that had been separated from its head. Had he sewn it on? Or did the dead girl hold it in her cold hands? Zoe had not particularly liked Isabel, whom she had seen day in and day out in their shared rooms. She had been too quiet, too dreamy. But when the priest talked about the magical world of Isabel's dreams, to which she now finally belonged, Zoe had cried.

And she had felt envy because Isabel had gotten to die. Zoe had longed for death for a long time. Very long, very strongly.

∽

The Line 2 streetcar was heading toward Günterstal, the remote and southernmost part of the city, under brooding, fickle skies. Once upon a time, it had been an independent village between the Black Forest hills. Three more stations, two more. Again the voice of danger: *Come closer!*

Her father had also said "Come closer" back then. When he still had words ready and did not let the belt speak. *Come closer!* her father had said, to teach her to walk in the communal garden in the backyard of the apartment block that could never match her mother's dreams—dreams of her home country in African. Zoe remembered the smell of her father. Of the eau de toilette that mixed with his sweat. He had smelled good, her father.

Back then, Zoe had stretched out her arms and wanted to go to him. But he had always taken a step backward.

As a little girl, she had a foot that curved slightly inward. As a result, the doctor had said she might not learn to walk easily.

But she had managed. She had wanted to. Desperately. Now she had a walk that drew attention, especially from the boys. That was good. That helped her with what she had to do.

The houses of Günterstal were drawing nearer. The streetcar passed through the archway of a former monastery.

Zoe got off. The last stop for today. She had almost made it. But she had to stay alert. Couldn't let herself get caught.

The afternoon sun moved behind veils like a traveler who doesn't want to be recognized.

A quick glance at the clock. Zoe was well ahead of time. In a moment, it would be recess and students would be streaming into the courtyard. She only had fifteen minutes, then she had to make her way back. Back to the village where she was stranded. Where the other teenagers lived. And the counselor was trying to take away their nasty, dark worries.

Want to get something off your chest?

No thanks, Zoe thought. *Also, screw you.*

The counselor thought that Zoe was at fencing practice, which happened three times a week. She hadn't realized that practice was canceled today. Zoe had not told her about it.

Zoe wanted to make the most of the time.

She walked down the streetcar platform. A station platform was a symbol of desperate waiting, Zoe thought.

A symbol of not being able to escape. No matter which streetcar you got on.

She climbed over the fence. She noticed how dirty her fingernails were, which annoyed her. Not because she was eager for cleanliness. But because clean fingernails provide that sweet lie that nothing remains of what one's hands have come into contact with. Hands can absolve themselves of what they have done, just like that.

But the boys, they didn't pay attention to fingernails. They were after something else. Her body, for example.

And what was hidden in the back pocket of her tight-fitting jeans.

She burrowed through the bushes and stepped out into the bright schoolyard, where every voice screamed like a trumpet and the scent of fear lingered in the air. *It's sweetish,* she thought. Like lilac, perhaps.

She walked around. As if she were a piece of cork floating in the current, a molecule belonging to the crowd. But the truth was different: she didn't belong here. This was not her school. And she didn't drift. She chose her steps deliberately. She was careful not to be seen. Or she was careful that certain people did see her . . . She took her usual position at the corner of the long gym hall. She immediately felt several pairs of eyes gawking at her. Shy, lonely eyes, distrustful of happiness. Her task was to remove all doubt. She knew the moves that lead boys toward happiness.

And she made it tangible, that happiness. It was the slightest movements of her body that distributed points of light. And the colors of her clothes, the earrings, the scarf in the storm of her hair—it all helped. And, of course, the smile, the conspiratorial smile on her face.

Little by little, they came, the boys. It was almost always them. Even when girls wanted something, they sent the boys ahead.

It was a good afternoon on the schoolyard in Günterstal.

She sold gossamer scraps that melt on the tongue and shift consciousness until every image, every place, seems like home.

Even the places that are dark, like the heart.

For the six students brave or hopeless enough to buy from her, it would come true—her promise of happiness. Hardworking students, Zoe thought. Even someone new had bought from her. A boy with a delicate face. Over the past few weeks, she had watched as the distance he kept from her gradually shrank. Until today, when she heard his voice for the first time, which was just as sweet. She tried not to let it affect her. All that mattered was the money he handed her. And that was no small amount.

Then recess was over. The students quickly disappeared into the school building. Zoe was left alone in the courtyard.

Alone? No, she was not alone.

Suddenly he was there: Fynn. Lurking Fynn from her group home.

Actually, his name was Fred. But Fred was really not the name for him. Much too harmless.

Fynn didn't go to school here any more than she did. But like her, he mainly hung around Freiburg to escape their small town, and he knew which schoolyards she frequented to conduct her little business. Actually, he went to a high school near Hofsgrund, and rarely showed up there.

He slowly approached her. His movements betrayed the supple power of muscles directed by a sharp, unyielding mind. His movements never had the jerky haste of strained nerves but the nimbleness of a cat. She saw his strong hands, which in spite of herself she wanted to feel on her skin again, the hands which had so often pulled off her clothes.

Fynn had raised the hood of his hoodie over his head, as he so often did, covering his face. Only his cold eyes gleamed out from under it. The hoodie was his trademark. With it, he wore pants that reached just below his knees. Even now, in November, he wore them, so you could see his tattooed legs. They were cool patterns. She had only belatedly realized that they also hid a swastika.

"Good business?" he asked. "Do you have a bite for me, too?"

"You know very well that I don't give out free samples," she said.

"But you usually offer me everything for free," he said. "My ace of spades."

Ace of *spades*. She frowned. Fynn so easily called her by that word.

He made no secret of the fact that he detested people like her. And any people who came from other countries. Even though his mother was a foreigner herself. He never tired of saying, *That bitch killed my father!* Zoe couldn't say for sure if the story was true. But her gut told her it was the truth. The whole thing had to have been very brutal. His mother had killed his father with a scythe. "What are you doing here?" she asked.

"Just chatting," he said. "Or can you think of anything else to do? After all, there's no one here. Maybe some fifth-graders might peek out the window." He grinned at her.

That was the basic requirement of their clandestine meetings—that no one they knew would be around. Fynn had made that abundantly clear. Over and over again, he would tell everyone around him that Zoe was the absolute worst. A foreign bitch. But she was good enough to screw in secret. He humiliated her with it. And somehow she let it happen.

In the beginning, it had been just an adventure for her. She would slip through a forbidden door. But she had not expected what had happened behind that door. She had, in a strange way, fallen for Fynn. As a little girl, she had often collected and eaten white, poisonous snowberries in the forest. She couldn't have said exactly why. The thrill was a part of it, of course. But also the hidden desire to harm herself. When she ate them, she had imagined the poison of the berries entering her bloodstream and taking hold of her being. It was the same with Fynn. He had long since penetrated deep into her innermost being. There was no turning back now.

"Sit down!" he said. They took a seat on a bench. From his pants pocket, he pulled out a silver thing that you put on your index finger, with a tip that was like a long, curved fingernail of sharpened metal. He played with it as he said, "It's almost time. We don't need to wait any longer."

"Good," Zoe said. Her mouth had gone dry. She knew the plan. She knew the promise she had made. Sometimes she had wondered if he really meant it. She hoped he did. She longed for it. She was not attached to life.

She thought of the poems they had studied in school. They had never interested her much. Only one had pleased her. By Robert Frost. It was called "Fire and Ice." She knew it by heart:

Some say the world will end in fire,
Some say in ice.
From what I've tasted of desire
I hold with those who favor fire.
But if it had to perish twice,
I think I know enough of hate
To say that for destruction ice
Is also great
And would suffice.

She remembered how she and Fynn had climbed one night up Castle Hill, which rose sprawling against the sky near the old town. How they had followed the winding paths between the trees until they had finally reached the tower with its long wooden trunks, which were set up around the steel staircase and reminded her of giant pick-up sticks. Step by step, they climbed up the narrow spiral staircase to the top observation deck. It had been windy and cold as shit up there. But she had barely felt that when Fynn tore down her pants and took her from behind, hastily and relentlessly. Below them the lights of the city, above them the moon, shredded by drifting clouds.

Afterward, Fynn had insulted her again and said that she was worthless. Like all of life. She had agreed with him. And then they had made the decision. To take their own lives together, one day.

Now the day was near. Zoe found she had a queasy feeling at the thought of it. She didn't like that. She wanted to be tough. Not harbor any doubts, not show any weakness. If there was even the slightest doubt before a fencing match, she knew she was already defeated. But Zoe was almost never defeated. Zoe was good. Zoe was strong. And yet, something had changed. She could feel it. Since when? She knew precisely when. Since Isabel died. Something had penetrated her consciousness. That maybe this fleeting life could be valuable after all. She told herself that a funeral was bound to make one emotional. She would get over it. Had to. Quickly.

"I think so," she said.

"I agree," Fynn said. "But what would you say if we changed our plan slightly?"

"What do you mean?"

"A little death, just two, like that, is a little pathetic, don't you think? Insignificant. It won't make any difference. Everything will go on afterward just as it was before. All the scum keeps spreading. Everything goes into a new round. It goes on and on. Do you really want that? I'm guessing no. Don't we want to do something big? Something really big?"

"What are you talking about?"

He pulled back the hood of his hoodie. He smiled.

"How about we take some others with us?"

"Are you stupid?"

"Don't act like you care about anyone." He sneered. "Save your phony act. You want them to die too, don't you? I know you do."

Zoe was silent. "Who did you have in mind?" she finally asked.

"Everyone," he said. "Everyone."

A pause.

"I saw it in my dream, exactly," he said. "I saw them die. It was beautiful. So beautiful. I know it's going to happen soon. We can be part of it, you and me. We can help make it so."

Zoe stared at him. He sounded like he had lost his mind. But she sensed he hadn't.

"How did you come with all this?"

"He told me. He talked about both of us, you and me."

"Who?"

"The man. The man who came out of the dark lake."

⁓

As Zoe walked back to the bus stop that afternoon, she felt exhausted. Her thoughts found no peace. The sky was completely overcast. The air possessed a piercing, wintry quality. No one seemed to be on the streets. It was as if the inhabitants had fled into their houses. But it was of no use to them. Zoe knew that. The only escape left for them was the one granted by death. Death gladly welcomed all those who fled.

Just before the stop, Zoe saw a small child coming toward her on the empty sidewalk. She could not have told if it was a boy or a girl. The child was wrapped in a strange blanket that was full of holes and tattered and much too large to handle. The blanket was made of coarse cloth that hung down in heavy folds. Around the child's head was a stained cloth made of cotton like a hood into which their face disappeared. Zoe had never seen anything like it. As the child came closer, Zoe saw how unsteady their steps were. She saw that they had no shoes on. Their bare feet looked sore, caked with dirt.

The child stopped in front of Zoe as if they had finally found their target.

"The others aren't here," she heard the little voice say. "My two brothers aren't, and neither is my sister, and neither are my mother and father. I am alone. I'm the only one here. We were going through the village. Looking for something to eat."

"This is not a village," Zoe said.

"Not now," the child said. "This is then. A very long time ago. I don't know when. I'm little. I don't know numbers. The houses were tiny then. The roads were muddy and full of dirt. The air stank. The night was very strong then. Torches and candles couldn't fight it. My family and I, with many others, went on a long march. There had been no harvest that year. Everything was flooded. There was hunger, hunger like burning in the belly. The others didn't last, even though they were all bigger than me. I was the youngest. Mama was still there in the end. But then she collapsed, and her cheeks sank in, and her body was completely stiff, and the October wind pulled at her to wake her up. But it did not work. She was taken to a meat house. That's where they dumped the corpses. They were overflowing with death. There were so many corpses in there. Without a blessing. Without a shroud. I didn't end up in a meat house. I followed a man into a dark doorway. He had promised to give me an apple. But the only apple to pick there was me. There was nothing left of me. I am small, after all. I am a child, after all. Where can we play? Tell me, where can all us children play?" With these words, the child, a girl, removed the cloth from her head. It was the saddest face Zoe had ever seen.

∽

That night, Zoe dreamed. She dreamed of children playing.

"Yo, can I finally get in?" She heard her roommate's voice outside the bathroom door early in the morning. Zoe had locked herself in. She stared, aghast, at a cross. At the small blue cross that had appeared on the pregnancy test. She closed her eyes and saw Fynn's face in front of her. Saw his cold eyes. Heard his voice:

"I saw it in my dream, exactly. I saw them die."

18

The colors at the Freiburg market brought back memories for Fynn. Especially now at this time of year, when the colors of nature had faded, and the black of winter lay in wait.

As a young boy, he had often immersed himself in the hustle and bustle of the market on Münsterplatz with his father. That is, with the man who had occasionally said, "Well, I'm your father, I guess." In a voice as hard as brass. He had been a cook in a second-rate Black Forest inn. But he had thought a lot of his cooking skills. He had shown Fynn how to recognize good fruit and vegetables. Which smells are crucial. Which degree of ripeness must be reached. Which color spoke the truth. He trusted the color green the most, although there were many exceptions.

One evening his mother had gone to the shed and fetched the scythe with which his father had often pruned the tall green grass in the back garden. She had hacked at him from behind until the red of his blood running across the stone floor of the patio spoke the truth.

The scythe had gone into evidence. And Fynn, the couple's only child, into a psychiatric clinic. He didn't give a shit what the psychologists did to him, though. But he did manage to persuade one of them, who was particularly naive, to stand up for him with a request. The psychologist drafted a letter explaining that it would be helpful for his young patient to be handed the murder weapon after the police investigation was completed. So that he could confront the horrific act directly and thus better process the traumatizing experience. The request was finally granted after some contentious discussions. The scythe came into Fynn's possession. He covertly kept it downstairs in the basement of the shared house. It was a prized possession. He was sometimes amused by the spiteful name he had given the scythe: Forget-Me-Not. He knew that one day it would be put to use. He didn't know on what occasion. But he had a feeling he wouldn't have to wait too much longer.

Pulling the hood far over his face, Fynn went on his way alone. He hated people and the pathetic bonds that kept them together. He hung out with only a few people his age, bumming a cigarette once in a while, dropping two or three words. That was enough. The other teenagers didn't understand why Fynn liked to roam the market. They thought it was ridiculous, or maybe it just meant that he was gay. He'd kicked the crap out of a couple of them for that. They didn't understand good food. They could fuck off with their sandwiches and burgers.

Yes, he liked this market, which was held every day except Sunday. Farmers and merchants from all over the surrounding area offered their wares under the cathedral that towered into the sky.

Fynn ate a long red, a bratwurst that could not be found anywhere else. He stopped by Stefan's stand, where there were excellent cheesecakes to choose from. His favorite was the one with chestnut mousse, which was always available starting in November.

But although this market was teeming with life, although scents and pleasures were omnipresent, Fynn always felt the proximity of death. And this was not only because of the bones of countless corpses beneath the cobblestones, which had been buried there in great numbers in the Middle Ages.

No, he knew that all the people around him were doomed to death. And that they deserved it. He smiled at the thought.

But then Fynn saw something. Something he didn't like. He saw the hands of a man.

"How many?" the man asked in labored German.

"Two," Fynn said.

He had picked out a salad recipe to try in the evening. A zucchini salad with onions, raspberries, and a vinaigrette into which he would mix some marmalade.

He watched the fingers of the man at the vegetable stand pawing the zucchini. Fynn didn't like those fingers. *They're groping for a happiness they don't deserve,* he thought.

Fynn knew the man these fingers belonged to. He had seen him many times. The guy lived in a home for asylum seekers. Fynn knew that from information gathered on his wanderings. His observations. The man had been carried in on one of those waves that were sweeping the country, now one of the people loitering there and wanting to be cared for. With their eyes full of phony neediness. And their hands reaching this way and that, just waiting for the opportunity to take possession of everything. That's what Fynn was thinking as he looked at the man's fingers. They were clean fingers. No dirt visible under the nails. Only a slight grayness to them. Clean fingers, yes. And yet, something unclean transferred to them onto the vegetables. He felt it clearly—no doubt about it.

The man's eyes questioned him uncertainly, asking if he wanted anything more. *These eyes have no business asking me anything,* Fynn thought. *The eyes should go away and not wander where they have no business. They'll go away, just like his fingers.*

Fynn turned to another merchant. Told him the guy was staining the vegetables with his filthy fingers. There was an irritated silence. Then the merchant managed a few words. Meek, offended, pathetic. Words that tried to preach at him but were only helpless. A market supervisor interfered. A rich university ass, whose mouth reeked of onions and who had nothing to say to him. When he got too close, Fynn gave him a slight push, and the guy fell backward to the ground.

And then they jumped on him—the whole phony mob. Fynn had been there before. He knew it all too well. When they had hold of him, Fynn shot another look at the man who lived in the refugee shelter. A look that told him what else was in store for him soon.

When the sun had set, it was time. Darkness had spread over the city. At the police station, he had played the good guy. He had been under too much stress, had overreacted—the whole bullshit. The police officers quickly let him go.

Fynn immediately returned to the market. By a streetcar as dark as any path that leads into the night. He arrived in time. The stalls and booths were still inviting people to buy. He had to wait for a little while. But that was not bad.

He was lucky. The guy from the refugee shelter was still there.

A short time later, Fynn smiled at him. Smiled down into the bloodied face sandwiched between his knees. Just as he was about to strike again, a man suddenly emerged from the shadows. Fynn recognized him immediately. It was the man he had been dreaming about over and over. The one who emerged from the dark waters of the lake and had called Fynn by name. All this time, the man would not leave his thoughts. Never before had Fynn felt so connected to someone. He had sensed what this man was capable of. Had sensed his plan and that Fynn was to play a significant role in it. It was the man with whom he would stand as he delivered death. Finally.

He even knew his name from his dreams. Tristan Nightsworn sat down on one of the benches that invited people to linger under chestnut trees here on the secluded square called Adelhauser Klosterplatz. The sulfurous yellow light of the streetlamps fell on the man's coat. Many residents of Freiburg appreciated this square and its fountain as a blissful place of tranquility. The former monastery facing the square was the color of oxblood. A sign that this quiet square was also ideally suited for violence, Fynn thought. Bottle shards flashed on the asphalt like little stars. Tristan Nightsworn's eyes locked on Fynn. Fynn wasn't sure he had ever been looked at in such a way. He felt noticed, respected, valued. With renewed vigor, he punched the asylum seeker's face, which was no longer a face.

And then the observer's voice, which he already knew from his dream, rang out. "You're doing quite well."

When Fynn let the blade of his jackknife spring open, the voice held him back. "Better to leave it at that! You're just wasting your precious strength here." The man rose and stepped close to him. "What do you want with this nothing of a blade anyway? You know you can do much better. You have something waiting in the basement. It has waited long enough. Now the scythe shall taste blood again. Lavishly. How does that sound?" the stranger asked.

It sounds good. Very good, Fynn thought.

19

The day constantly changed its name. First, it called itself Friday, then Saturday, then Sunday. When its name was Sunday, then it would be time. Time to kill.

The young man never changed his name. He didn't need to. Whatever happened, he was always Henry B. Lindt, twenty-three years old.

Do you want to see my ID? No? No one had ever asked him for his ID after those rare Sundays that were his joy. Never had anyone been able to accuse him of anything. The reason: he had always been but a fleeting visitor, disappearing as quickly as he had come. He changed locations, and the skies above him changed, and he would still be Henry B. Lindt, in his early twenties. And free. At large.

This time he had chosen Freiburg im Breisgau.

He had never been here before. He found the city, surrounded by the hills of the Black Forest, to be a natural beauty, with its medieval center and towering Gothic cathedral. It had taken three centuries to complete this masterpiece of architecture. Construction had begun in the Romanesque style and was completed in the Gothic and late Gothic styles.

The streets of the old town were paved with split Rhine pebbles and were crisscrossed by the Bächle, water channels flowing through the streets, that had existed there since the twelfth century. In the past, they had served as watering places for cattle, had provided water for firefighting, and also the residents had thrown their garbage into them. Henry liked the idea that there had always been body parts among the garbage. Meanwhile, the gutter streams were popular with children who launched small model boats there.

Yes, Freiburg might be beautiful. Nevertheless, the city would be easy to let pass into mental oblivion. Henry Lindt was skilled at forgetting places.

One should not become attached to places, not even mentally. Henry knew that clinging meant being discovered.

He would follow his usual pattern, have a few lovely, leisurely days. A long weekend, so to speak. It started on Thursday with a trip and would end in blood on Sunday.

He had arrived in the afternoon and had wandered undetected through the alleys of the old town until daylight faded. The streetlamps shimmered on the cobblestones. The many-shaped devils, gargoyles, and other mysterious stone creatures that sat on the flanks of the cathedral and fascinated him slowly faded into darkness.

His lodging was a small boarding house on Fischerau, a tiny alley that was charming to look at. There were some remarkable houses there. They leaned against each other and looked out over the gently rippling water of a narrow commercial canal.

He had chosen this address for a reason. A few centuries ago, this alley, then just outside the gates of the city proper, had not been so charming. People lived tightly packed together in squalor. The alley had been home to a woman who was burned as a witch. A little cruelty like that was nice to put one in the mood, he thought.

When he entered the boarding house, he pretended to have a physical disability. A handicapped person would clearly be less likely to have perpetrated an act of terror.

He had the man at the front desk carry his only piece of luggage into the room. A narrow, oblong bag equipped with a carrying strap. Really not that heavy.

He smiled at the thought that the man had no clue what was inside it.

⌇

The following day he strolled to a brothel located near the Swabian Gate, one of the medieval gates into the city, in a house that looked decidedly respectable and radiated righteousness. He had a good fuck. Afterward, he took the woman, who called herself Francine, to the boarding house and introduced her as his sister. It was supposedly because of her that he had come to town. Admittedly, his sister dressed a bit revealingly. But someone who visited his pathetic sister had to be a nice person, right? It was good to be Henry B. Lindt. Lucky to have had that distinguished, ambitious, oh-so-smart father. That father who had died just in time. And had—as was proper—bequeathed his enormous wealth from his pharmaceutical company to his son, the only remaining relative.

So that he could do what he wanted. The son did not do much. He did little. And what he did was traveling. Strolling. What he did was extinguish life—a little hobby. Every third month, it would be that time. He would go to a place he didn't know and select a single victim. He never knew the people he chose. They were utter strangers to him. Just as he was unknown.

It was bliss to be Henry B. Lindt. To look out into the day from seawater-blue eyes, to move smoothly through the streets with his slender, graceful body. Wearing a smile that was like an invitation to dance.

But the bliss, lately? He had noticed that he had grown tired—grim, melancholy. The irrepressible anger that had been in him since childhood was demanding more and more space. He became aware of what should always have been obvious. In truth, there was no happiness. Nowhere. His fleeting sparks of elation were not enough, not to wish a miserable death on the entire world. More and more often, he wished death on himself as well.

What had been Friday, what had been Saturday, passed. Sunday was unfolding. Henry had made the most of his time. Had familiarized himself with the city and had also already chosen his victim. A young guy with pocked skin who worked in a bakery on a quiet streetcorner in the Herdern neighborhood. The bakery, he already knew, would close at half-past twelve that day. He had already checked out of the boarding house. He would wait patiently until the young clerk, who stood alone every day behind the narrow counter, unsuspectingly went off work.

He would stroll along behind him, his narrow bag slung casually over his shoulder. It looked like it had a flute or something in it. But that was not what was in it. It was an instrument of death: a rapier. This rapier had once belonged to the general Albrecht von Wallenstein, who had enriched himself on death and misery during the gloom of the Thirty Years' War.

On his twentieth birthday, Henry had gifted himself with this extraordinary weapon, which he simply called Battlelord. A museum in Berlin had offered it in an under-the-table sale for a large sum. They had secretly replaced the original in the museum display with a duplicate. The rapier had not been cheap. But it had been worth the money. He had worked on the weapon himself so that it was perfectly suited to his deadly needs.

Henry knew how to handle his weapon. During his childhood, he had practiced handling cutting and stabbing weapons. He had taken part in German youth championships. He kept himself in shape. He lost count of the number of beefy guys who had tried to take him on and who had failed. Failed because of his speed, his will, and his hatred. He kept in shape. In every way. Even for killing.

Sunday was the best day for killing. Everything was quiet. Few people showed themselves on the streets. And if they did, they were sleepy, inattentive. Depressed by the heaviness of the approaching beginning of the week. A gray Sunday in autumn was particularly suitable.

The bakery salesman made it easy for him. He didn't have a bike, which would have meant Henry couldn't have followed him on foot. Nor did he get into a car. Henry smiled because his assessment had been correct. He had predicted that this guy was a lonely walker. He was amused by the way he walked. As if something was stuck to his shoe.

It was almost too easy. It presented no challenge. Then, on top of everything, the guy wandered right through the middle of the Old Cemetery, where not a single person was to be seen.

The Old Cemetery was a hidden treasure of the city. Ancient trees, wildly sprawling meadows and shrubs, where graves, paths, and walls bore the patina of times past.

Henry had inspected the cemetery the day before and listened to the whispering voices of the dead.

He had been particularly taken with a stone skull that was part of a grave pedestal. He had read that the skull was in memory of a master blacksmith killed by his young wife and her lover. They had driven a nail into his head as he slept.

Yes, this venerable place appealed to him.

Henry quickened his pace, getting closer and closer to the young man. He casually took his bag off his shoulder as he walked. Calmly, without rushing, he quietly unzipped it and pulled out the rapier. His fingers slipped into the grip and guard artfully fashioned from fine rings, clasps, and hoops that served to protect his hand. It was a delicate moment and the most exciting of all. Once the weapon was visible, and he could be discovered. But only in theory. Henry was vigilant.

In his mind's eye, he already saw how he would wipe the blood from the blade afterward with the beautiful silk cloth he always had with him. The whole affair would be over in a minute or two at most. The bakery clerk advanced deeper into the shadows of tall trees. The time had come.

It would be quick . . .

But then Henry stopped abruptly. He let the young man walk on with his strange gait, five yards, ten, fifteen. Henry paused in the shade of the trees. His mind was working feverishly. He had a sudden feeling that he was being watched. Something was lurking behind him. He sensed a threat drawing nearer and nearer. Then he heard a voice. It reached him from a distance of a few steps away yet felt as if it were penetrating his innermost being.

"Isn't this shop boy a little beneath you? We both know what Henry B. Lindt is capable of."

Turning around in irritation, he first saw a strange bluish light gleaming among the graves. Then he spotted the two figures moving toward him. One was a man wearing a cloak that was drawn tightly around his slender waist. The second was a younger man in a hoodie that covered his face in shadows. Although it was very chilly, the young man's pants reached just below his knees. Henry hated guys like that, who wore hoodies and shuffled around as if they were following some secret plan but were really just dull, lazy assholes.

Then, in the pale light of the cemetery, he made a discovery that unnerved him. He saw that the man was holding a sword in his right hand. Henry had never seen such a sword before. It had a curved blade and appeared to be old, very old, and yet there was no doubt that this sword was capable of flooding the earth with the blood at any moment. The teenager carried a scythe with a slightly shortened handle of black metal and a blade that made him shiver.

"With whom do I have the pleasure?" asked Henry, trying to appear as composed as possible.

"With two men you should meet." The the voice that had spoken before belonged to the older man.

"I'm not interested," Henry countered.

"Of course, you can go on pursuing your hobby of killing pathetic little shits. We're not going to stop you. Somehow, though, I have a feeling you're capable of more. Such a miniscule death is meager fare for a hunter, isn't it?"

Henry stayed motionless. He kept the rapier low to the ground, ready to attack at any moment. He tried to fathom what these two figures who had suddenly appeared were after, but he could not. Apparently, they had known in advance that he could be found in this place. What's more, they even seemed to know who he was and what he had intended to do. They knew his name.

He wondered if he had crossed their paths before. He possessed an excellent memory but could not recall ever having seen them.

The choice of their weapons—scythe and sword—represented an uncanny connection to his own weapon.

This was, after all, the twenty-first century. Persons facing each other with ancient weapons were not so common. He had the uncanny feeling that these two characters had something in common with him.

"What do you want?" he asked.

"We have come to admit you into a closed society," said the teenager, whose face he could now make out. It looked menacing, with eyes that revealed unwavering darkness.

"But I may not want to join," Henry said.

"We'll see . . ."

Henry hesitated no longer. In a flash, he moved toward the teenager, head lowered, rapier outstretched to ram the tip of the blade into the body of his opponent. But the young fellow reacted immediately, deflecting the blow. Then he leapt toward Henry, throwing his strength into his arm, swinging the scythe. Henry dodged. He held the rapier low to the ground for two seconds, then thrust it forward, aiming at his opponent's knee. The weapon stabbed into thin air. Then he felt something cold slide along his side. The scythe blade could have sliced him open. But he had moved just in time and prevented a worse injury. And it didn't hurt. When a blade enters flesh, you don't feel it, not at first. Henry thrust with his weapon again.

Henry didn't know how long the fight ultimately lasted. His vision began to darken. He had a feeling of being in the vastness of the sky, but sky and earth had switched positions. The two combatants found themselves lying on damp leaves, moaning in pain. Both had several gaping wounds that oozed blood. Henry looked over at the man in the blue coat. The man in the blue coat looked down at him.

"I thought you two would be a good match," he said. "This fine young man's name is Fynn, by the way. You're going to see much together. You fought well, my fiend. It was nice watching you. But you feel a little tired, don't you? Would you say a tiredness of heart? Or maybe more like tired of life? I know you're ready to die, Henry B. Lindt. You have been for a long time. But why keep death away while you turn the color of a tired old lime yourself? Why doesn't your hatred laugh louder? Why doesn't it laugh so loudly that everyone can hear it? The fearful, the desperate. Why isn't your hatred laughing the way God and the devil laugh when they bargain for souls? Why be so stingy with death?" After a brief pause, he added, "Let me introduce myself. My name is Tristan Nightsworn." Henry looked into the man's eyes and thought he saw something that made his violent, melancholy longing, his whole existence, culminate in one great purpose.

"What is this about?" he asked, still panting to regain his breath.

"At the moment, I'm trying to assemble some talent."

"Talent for what?"

"To start something."

"Like what?" asked Henry.

"The end of the world."

20

Hofsgrund lay in the shadow of the blue-black mountains that rose all around in. Fynn sat on the bench by the bus stop and looked up the narrow path, which was inadequately lit by a few streetlamps. The bus stop was the only spot anywhere nearby that was halfway bearable. He often loitered there because this was the place that best expressed his feelings: *I don't belong here. I don't belong with you. I want to leave. Fuck all of you!* He still felt sore from the injuries from his fight yesterday. Not a bad fighter, this Henry B. Lindt. Fynn liked him, actually. The guy was casual. Elegant. Mercilessly evil. You could tell that he came from a wealthy family and had strolled through countless fancy doors, but that that didn't seem to have made much of an impression on him.

On the contrary, it had instead made him bored. Sometimes it just did not take much to become a cold-blooded killer. Sometimes boredom was enough.

Fynn hadn't put much effort into bandaging his wounds. He was tough. And he liked the feeling of having the marks of violence on his body. He liked to beat a guy until he was sure he could feel his own hands swelling.

Fynn sat at the bus stop and watched her come down the hill, right at him. Saw her dipping into the circle of a streetlamp.

She was good-looking. Sexy. The ace of spades. *His* ace of spades. No one else was in sight.

Zoe had wanted to see him. Desperately. She had something on her mind. Fynn knew what it was about. He chose the place for to meet up, as always.

He looked at his hands. He held a life between those hands. His hands were strong. Life was weak.

He thought back to that morning. He had gone to school again for a change. He had even enjoyed it. In class, they had talked about the forest. About how the roots of the trees spread and branched out in the moist, loose soil. And how they could absorb water with the fine hairs that formed all around the roots. The teacher had gotten all excited talking about the breath of the trees, about the countless tree-mouths on the underside of a single leaf. Fynn had listened with amusement at the way everything and everyone clung so desperately to life! The foul-sweet smell of fermenting fruit hit his nose, wafting from the backyard of the old Adler inn. The streetlamps trembled slightly in a rising wind. Dim light seeped from lace-covered windows.

Zoe approached the bus stop bench. He sensed her restlessness. Sensed how nervous she was. Stepping from one leg to the other. Incessantly. He didn't care. He had no interest in releasing her from this nervousness. He didn't lift his eyes, stayed looking at the faint life between his fingers. Thinking about how much living creatures all resembled each other.

"You're late," he said.

"Fynn, I have something to tell you. It's important." He sensed she was struggling with herself. He had sensed her fear of him when he'd first started going after her. He could tell that she found it hot, that fear. He could tell that her fear of him had grown even more. That pleased him. He knew how fear created attraction. The more you feared a person, the stronger the pull from that person. It was a thing he had taken advantage of with Zoe from the beginning.

"I know what you're trying to tell me," he said.

She looked at him with wide eyes. "You know? How?"

"As you know," he said, "we have a new friend: Tristan Nightsworn. He wants the best for both of us—for you, and for me. And he a good eye for things—extremely good. So I already know about it from Tristan. And it's stupid of you to think it would make any difference. We made a promise to each other, remember?" Now he looked up.

"Look!" he said. He raised his hands in the air so she could see the little bundle of fur he held between his fingers—a kitten.

"I got it earlier from an old woman who had a litter to give away. She just gave it to me, just like that. She said: I'm sure the kitten will do well with you. Just look how it curled up in your hands . . ." For a moment, Zoe seemed unsettled. Flustered. But as was her way, she quickly shook it off. At least, she made it seem that way.

"It doesn't take a cat," she said, "to show me what kind of guy you are or remind me about our promise. Leave it alone!"

He looked calmly into Zoe's eyes. "You care about this creature, don't you? Feel for it. Can't blame you. It's adorable." He gently set the animal down on the ground. "I'll let it go." As the kitten made its way clumsily across the quiet street toward the sheltering doorway of someone's home, maybe its new home, he added, "But we both know what that thing is going to find out there sooner or later. What everything has to find: death."

21

It was a long way from Schleiermoos Farm to St. Margaret's. About seven miles in a northeasterly direction. With many twists and turns, often going uphill. Through an almost impassable area far from any town. Through thorns and brushwood, in the deep shadows of the trees. Daniel had never taken the path before, and although he was familiar with the places of worship in the area he had not heard of this chapel. Probably because it was so secluded, he thought. A mysterious place in the middle of the forest. Mysterious and eerie.

Daniel hadn't known about the chapel until after Isabel's death, when people talked about how she liked to go there.

He hadn't been able to set off until afternoon. Before that, he had been tied up with school, farm, homework, cooking. His mother had gone with his brothers to visit his father in the hospital. Or rather, his brothers taken with their mother. All together, except Daniel and Balder. Who was out there, somewhere. In the darkness.

Their mother was barely responsive. Her eyes no longer seemed to register what was happening in front of them. They seemed to see something else: the creature that had invaded the dining room a few days before, leaving their father in a pool of blood. Remains of the blood were still visible in the cracks of the wooden floor.

All the same, their mother must be glad that she was free of him for the time being. Daniel had not visited him yet. He felt guilt, but that made no difference. He wished his father a miserable death.

He crossed himself as he thought of it. *Hey, Daniel, have you prayed the rosary today? Will the Lord heal you even if I beat the shit out of you?* That was how the other kids often talked to him. He tried to get those voices out of his head. He made wide detours so he wouldn't be seen when he went to church early in the morning to pray before school started. It didn't help, though. He was spotted often enough. And often enough, praying didn't help a bit.

But on that afternoon on the lonely forest paths, there was no one to ambush him—actually. Daniel knew that wasn't true. He might not have to worry about random teenagers. But perhaps something else. Something far more terrifying.

He had tried to read up on the little chapel. Instructions on how to get there contradicted each other. Phones were no help in the dense Black Forest, where you lost reception as early along the trail. But Daniel trusted his local knowledge, trusted his intuition.

Fear rushed through his blood. *I will not give up,* he thought. He had a goal, and he would reach it. It was important.

He had a vague hope of finding clues in the chapel as to why such a terrible fate had befallen Isabel and Balder. Perhaps even how he might be able to help Balder. Even if only through prayer.

His brother was still alive, after all. But Daniel could only guess what such a life meant and to horror it would be capable of. He had to be strong, had to prevent what could be prevented.

At first, Daniel's path led uphill, across open fields. The rays of the setting sun hit a low bank of clouds, coloring them partly pink, partly scarlet. The sun sank further toward the horizon. He saw far-off valleys coming together at an acute angle, each with their villages and houses. And all around him, hills in the distance, towering up into mountains. The last light fell on brittle grass.

Then he penetrated deeper into the wood, where there was hardly any light and black lacy branches merged with the darkness of the sky.

Daniel thought of a classmate who had been in his class at Bartholomae Herder Lower School until ninth grade. Her name was Kathryn, but everyone called her Crow. She had helped him many times. Had saved him from being beaten up. She had been wiry and fast, an athlete who had played soccer since childhood. She had enormous strength and hadn't been afraid to take on tough guys to defend him. Daniel hadn't understood exactly why she'd done what she did. They didn't have much in common. Crow was rough and taciturn. And she had an unusual hobby: she stole stuff.

Once, when she had stolen a cab driver's bulging wallet, he had even been her accomplice. He had provided the distraction and had been scared shitless for weeks afterward. Remorse plagued him. A person who was supposed to stand up for the love of God could not let himself be drawn into that sort of thing. But Crow had been his friend, who had often helped him out of trouble. He could not refuse.

Shortly after that, Crow had suddenly stopped coming to school. At first, no details were given, only that she was ill. Then, after some time, word got around that she was in a psychiatric clinic for adolescents. The reason for it caused a big fuss. Crow had committed an *act of violence*. A *crime of passion*. On a summer night so hot that the air trembled as if it came from a monstrous furnace. The school year ended, and Crow had not returned. There was a rumor that she had dropped out entirely. Daniel had often thought of visiting her in the clinic. But he never did. Not even once. He had been too much of a coward. Too cowardly to look into the dark. He was ashamed of it. Now he thought about how there was no one he'd have wanted by his side more than Crow.

The path stretched on. Daniel was exhausted. Once, he rested at an old wayside shrine and asked the silence whether God was with him. God, as was usual, did not answer.

After another stretch of road, Daniel could see a group of yews and cypress trees ahead. His eyes had by now become quite accustomed to the darkness. He walked to the edge of the grove and saw that it was enclosed by a low wall. Finally, he found an opening through which he could slip. Behind it, the gloomy trees formed a very narrow path, which Daniel followed until he discovered the chapel's walls between the dense branches in a clearing.

As he approached the chapel, Daniel suddenly felt an icy cold.

And he felt something else. That he was no longer alone. The air was filled with movement. A kind of sighing could be heard. Voices began to whisper. For a moment, he thought he saw a pale face among the trees. Then a sweet chorus of psalms, sung by women's voices, rippled through the space. The voices seemed to be close to him, but he did not see the singers.

He quickly ran to the chapel door. Only now did it occur to him that it might be locked. How stupid of him not to think of that before! The bright voices seemed to follow him.

The narrow portal had no handle. Daniel pressed himself against the wood. It gave way and opened inward.

Quickly he closed it behind him, sliding a rough latch shut. Panic-stricken, he breathed in and out.

It was silent inside. Candles flickered as if someone had just been here. It smelled of incense, and he felt the chill of centuries. Daniel dipped his fingertips into the bowl of holy water and crossed himself. The altar lay steeped in shadow. Suddenly he could hear it again: the singing. It rang inside the chapel, echoing off its narrow walls. Then something seemed to come out of the shadows, emerging from dark corners. Daniel's blood pounded in his veins.

They approached him from all sides, ghostly creatures that he could not see but could only hear. Daniel wanted to flee. But when he turned around, there was a woman blocking his way. She stood directly in front of him in the dim light cast by the candles. Daniel stared at her. His confused gaze saw a slender body that seemed to be covered only by a delicate tissue-thin veil. Only after a few seconds did he realize that the woman was wearing a suit that clung tightly to her skin and shimmered in copper tones. Daniel had never seen anything like it. Then he spotted a long sword that the woman carried in a holster on her back. The woman's eyes were fixed on him.

He was sure he was doomed. There would be no getting past her. The ghostly creatures would tear him to pieces . . .

A strand of her curly hair fell across her forehead as she said, "You need not be afraid of them. They won't hurt you." And in fact, the spirit creatures did not come too close to him. He still felt their presence, heard their singing. But the singing grew quieter until it sounded only like a soft wind whispering.

"They can never be seen," the beautiful woman said in a quiet voice. "You can only ever hear them . . . They were once seven sisters. A long time ago, there was another church here. The sisters had taken shelter there all alone when Hun horsemen came and burned the villages. Trying to save his own life, a villager told the warriors where the sisters had gone to escape. The warriors stormed the church and raped them. And when the warriors left, the men bolted all the windows and the church door. The sisters were trapped. They kept singing their song. They sang it over and over again until, one by one, they died. Many times I've heard them. I heard their singing when I was a little girl. I visited them again and again in the old church. And later, much later, I also escaped there to hide. All alone. But it didn't do me any good either."

"Who are you?" asked Daniel.

"My name is Martha von Falkenstein," she said.

Daniel looked into her eyes, which were half-hidden under long silky lashes. He didn't know what to say. "When was that?" he finally stammered. "When was that, when you were hiding in the old church?"

Martha smiled. "Over eight centuries ago," she said.

"So you're a ghost, like those sisters?" asked Daniel after another silence.

"I am like them, and yet I am not. Unlike them, blood flows in my veins. And in my chest beats a heart. I am not a shroudless soul, wandering restlessly and lost through centuries. Martha von Falkenstein—the woman I once was—was long dead, but she has returned. I have become a human being again. With all my flaws. All of the vulnerability. I can die anew. Die just like you. But I do have some special abilities. A kind of sixth sense, if you will. For example, I can sense that you're about to wet your pants in fear."

"You don't need a sixth sense for that," Daniel said. Tentatively, he returned her smile.

"I sense something else," Martha said. "The strength that is within you. With which you bravely defend yourself against all your fear."

Suddenly there was complete silence in the chapel. The singing had stopped. Daniel no longer felt the presence of the ghost sisters.

"Come!" Martha said. "And I will show you something."

⌒

A stone portal opened in the wall. Martha and Daniel climbed a narrow rotten staircase. Daniel stayed close behind the woman. He watched her movements, full of strength and grace.

"What's that suit you're wearing?" he asked.

"I received it from the sisters," she said. "It's made of the petals of Copper Queen, a special rose. This suit is to protect me. As much as it can."

"Protect you from what?" asked Daniel. Martha did not answer.

They climbed up to the space under the gloomy vaulted roof of the chapel, which smelled of mildew, dust, and damp wood. At first, Daniel could discern nothing in the darkness. Then there was a light. It came from a roughly cube-shaped block of stone. As they drew closer, Daniel saw that it was an altar. On it, like an offering, lay a long sword that gave off a glow but seemed to be made entirely of copper. The metallic sheen of the weapon and the colors of Martha's suit harmonized with each other.

Daniel sensed that the ghostly beings were present again. He felt them roaming around the altar, heard their soft whispers.

Martha said, "Over the centuries, the chant of the seven sisters has given shape to this sword. For a long, long time, it remained hidden here. Now it is yours . . . if you choose to have it."

"Mine?" he asked. "Why? What do you mean?"

"It is yours if you choose to stand with me. If you choose to overcome your fear, and to fight. If you choose to be one of the Eight."

⌒

Daniel ran. He didn't know how he had gotten down the stairs so fast and found his way out of that gloomy chapel. Didn't know where he was running. His heart pounded

– 144 –

violently against his ribs, as if it wanted to burst out of his body, to free itself as Daniel himself had just freed himself. But had he really freed himself? He couldn't tell. He hoped the forest would throw its cloak of darkness over him, protect him. But, no matter how fast he ran, he couldn't seem to escape the chapel. Couldn't seem to escape this woman. Her words had pierced deeply into his consciousness.

Again and again, he heard her voice: "You know the man who killed Isabel," Martha had said.

∽

I know you saw him. I know he carries the sword the two of you found, your brother and you. The blade bears the name Xanas. I know your brother is with him and that he handed him the sword. That man is my adversary. He, too, has awakened from death and returned. We were chosen from among all the many souls. Why us two, I cannot say. It is a decision made in mysterious spheres into which we have no insight. But this man and I now have a task to fulfill. We cannot escape it. It has been inscribed in our hearts. We will fight each other soon. But it is not our fate that is at stake. It is the fate of this world.

The end of this world will be averted or sealed in battle. My adversary and I will not fight it alone. We must find allies. Ultimately, there must be eight fighters to compete against each other. No more, no less. Maybe you know that the eight is the number of the cosmic balance. A balance that is constantly put to the test.

How many of the eight fighters line up for one side, how many for the other, remains to be seen. Four against four, two against six, anything is possible. Either side can gain a possibly decisive advantage. Only one thing is certain. In the end, the fight will be under the sign of the Eight: eight fighters, eight souls, one fate. Either the world survives, or it will die.

I don't want her to die. I have returned to fight for her.

Will you be by my side, Daniel?

≈

Panic had seized Daniel. The feeling of being trapped in a nightmare. But then he had felt something else even more terrifying: that this was not a nightmare at all.

No, he had experienced everything in real life, in the flesh. His eyes had been open, his mind wide awake. He believed that this woman was telling the truth. Even if this truth could not be reconciled with anything he knew, anything he could even imagine.

He thought of his brother and what had happened to him. Martha had spoken of Balder as a matter of fact. Seemed to know what darkness had come over him. The same darkness that Martha would have to fight against. Against which he would also have to fight. Maybe his brother could still be saved. But how could Daniel be a fighter? He hated fighting. He hated weapons. He didn't think they were cool or anything. They scared him.

On top of that, he was a weakling, clinging to a God who . . . maybe didn't exist, something whispered inside him. A God who had never stood by him in the past. Not when his brother's monster awoke, and not when it attacked their father. Nor would He help Daniel now. How was Daniel supposed to take on a sword like the one Martha had wanted to hand to him? And how would he ever use a thing like that? Daniel saw blood in his mind's eye. Blood dripping from a long blade. And the image of the man in the long coat. Smiling.

Daniel ran and ran. He heard the rattle of his breath. Felt the dryness of his throat. Despite the cold that pervaded the forest, sweat poured down his face.

No, he would not be one of this Eight. He was barely even a one-half.

Whatever was meant to happen would happen. He could not change it.

He had come to a clearing. Moonbeams penetrated the black clouds and lit up the night. The wind whispered in the trees.

Suddenly the air seemed to be suffused with a gleam that came closer and closer. A face floated above him, surrounded by gloom. It was white and translucent, and its steady eyes were fixed on him.

It was Isabel

Her sad beautiful eyes looked at him. Her lips that he had dreamt of kissing parted. He heard her pleading voice: "Daniel—you must not give up!"

There was no longer any doubt. In that moment, he knew what he had to do. He had to turn around and return to the chapel. He had to take the sword and fight. He could not abandon Martha, and he could not abandon his brother. He could not let evil triumph without a fight. He could not abandon hope.

Martha was sitting in one of the narrow pews when Daniel entered the candlelit chapel. She glanced at him over her shoulder.

"I'm very glad you came back," she said, "and I'm grateful to you from the bottom of my heart." She rose and came toward him. In her hands was the copper-colored sword she had shown Daniel under the vaulted roof. She handed it to him.

"It doesn't have a name yet," she said. "What are you going to call it?"

Carefully, Daniel's fingers closed around the sword's hilt. The grip felt firm and supple. The sword didn't weigh as much as he had assumed. It felt good in his hand. It followed his slightest movements in a very pleasing way. Tentatively, his fingertips ran along the sharp blade. He glanced at Martha.

"Why me?" he asked.

"Because you're the only one," she said, "who can match your brother."

A shiver came over him as he thought of Balder. When he thought of fighting the creature he had become. Of fighting witth that sword.

"I'll call it Beloved Brother," he said.

As the two stepped out of the chapel into the cool night air, Daniel asked, "This man who killed Isabel and who you call your adversary—who is he?"

"He is the man I once loved," she said. And then she began to talk. She told him everything.

22

The longer he was back among the living, the more he began to feel. All the emotions returned to him. Even the feelings he had once banished into the darkness. Feelings of doubt, of powerlessness. And the feeling of guilt.

Two kinds of guilt existed in the world.

One was the guilt of loving. And one was the guilt of killing love.

Tristan Nightsworn knew again what it meant to be human.

He stood in the portico of the cathedral, looking at the depiction of Judgment Day on the magnificent tympanum above the entrance portal. This was the right place, he thought—the right place for the end.

He stepped inside the great cathedral.

The early Mass, which was held in the morning from seven to half-past, had just ended. The first prayers of the day faded into the deep silence, as so many had before.

His footsteps rang out as he walked across the hard square stone slabs of the nave.

Suddenly he stopped. He felt them. Felt the colors of the finely crafted stained glass on the north and south sides of the nave—a delicate glow in the stony coolness of the marvelous structure.

The memory rushed back. He saw images before him from centuries before when, as a very young man, he had pulled open the doorway of another church and pushed his way through. It had been the small stone church of St. George on the left bank of the Lower Rhine. He was expected to kneel in that austere chappel in prayer the night before he was to be sworn to the sword. In those days, it was one's sacred duty to spend the night before being knighted kneeling in a place consecrated to God. A fighter was a servant to his master—his king or his commander— but above all, he was a servant of God.

As his eyes had slowly adjusted to the dim light of the church, he had seen another young man kneeling in the choir, who seemed to be the same age as himself, and who had the same task to perform that night. Whispering, Tristan had introduced himself, after which the other had given his name in a soft voice: Albrecht von Falkenstein. Tristan had knelt down beside him on the hard floor, his eyes fixed on the narrow arched windows through which the soft light of the early evening fell. From outside, the chants of his feasting companions had been faintly audible. They were to move on the following day, along the Rhine and the Rhone to Marseilles, from which they were to embark for Outremer with the great goal of retaking the Holy Land.

The night hours in St. George passed, but Tristan had not fulfilled his duty. He had not prayed. Again and again, he had looked at the other young man out of the corner of his eye. He had sensed something. Something he would later call fate.

The person who knelt beside him that night was not

Albrecht von Falkenstein. It was a woman. A young woman from a poor background who had disguised herself as a man. Who had only pretended to belong to the noble house of Falkenstein. Martha.

Her courage, her beauty, and her fighting skills had impressed him. He had helped her so that she would not be discovered. He gave her a handsome horse. He gave her the equipment she needed for her long journey. Unlike Martha, Tristan actually came from a noble family. An ancient noble family that had once owned the mighty fortress called Xanas.

Together they went to war. The days had changed color. Red like blood. Red like love. They had sworn to stay together forever. Had sworn they would never stop fighting. Never stop loving. But one day, he had not been able to tell the difference between those two things. Again and again, he had wanted to prepare for battle. He wanted her by his side. But she refused. She had seen enough death. Her soul longed for life, and a life was growing in her womb. His child.

She had betrayed him. He had not wanted the child. He wanted only the two of them, Martha and him, no one else. She had made an oath! That they would both remain warriors until death. In the end, Martha had not died a warrior. She had died in flames as a heretic. He had seen to that. He was there when the fire ate her body. He had heard her screams. He still heard them long after. They haunted him as he wandered helplessly from place to place, succumbing to madness. And now he saw again the little face of a newborn in a foreign village, that he had slain with Xanas because he could not bear the baby's cries.

He saw a distant summer evening before him, when he had stood on the shore of Lake Flint, and the light in the sky had slowly faded, leaving only a blue that settled on the surface of the lake until the water had seemed thoroughly permeated by it. He saw before him how he—holding Xanas in his hand—had waded into the liquid blue, farther and deeper, until there had been no more ground beneath him and the water crashed over him. Thus had he put an end to his life.

Tristan knew he had to shake off all these memories and feelings. He had to focus on the hatred inside him that had brought him back to this life. He had received an imperative from higher powers. A punishment? He didn't know. All he knew was that he would prove himself worthy of that command. Martha was a woman. Just a woman. Even if one he had once known and on whom he had lavished his love.

She would be helpless against him, or the allies who fought at his side. He already had an excellent army. His army would continue to grow. The battle of the Eight would be decided quickly. No one could stop it. The end was near.

He strode down the nave of the cathedral and turned off into the south aisle until he reached the choir entrance. He slipped through the entrance and stepped into a small, darkened vault. There he found what he had come to see, to prepare himself for the last of all battles: the great sandstone slab set into the floor that looked as if it sealed the entrance to a medieval tomb, a slab in the shape of an octagon. Many people believed that there was a secret passage behind this stone, built by the princely dynasty of the

Zähringers. Tristan knew better. He knew that this stone was a gate and knew also what hid behind it.

Death.

More precisely: the winged army of the dead, which would bring about the end. When the battle of the Eight was decided, the two swords, Aurin and Xanas, would be united, and a key would be born from them. That key would unlock the stone behind which death hid, or it would lock it forever.

As he surveyed the octagon, Tristan saw figures appear on the stone—as if suddenly created by an invisible hand. On the left side were two humans, and on the right Tristan could make out four monstrous creatures about to pounce.

He smiled. So there were to be six. So six fighters had been chosen. And four of them were on his side. Martha had only won over a single ally. He guessed who: a weakling. She would have a hard time convincing any others. Tristan had been clever in his approach. Evil had the winning argument. Today, his team would prove to him that they were ready for battle. Ready to go to any extreme. He fully expected them to. He knew they would not disappoint him.

But suddenly, Martha's face appeared before his eyes again. He sensed that she, too, had been here only recently, also to get a glimpse of this stone and to learn how many fighters Tristan Nightsworn had already summoned. He saw Martha's face, which once he had loved. And he thought of the child, his child, who had died cruelly together with Martha. That child, too, would belong to the flying army of the dead.

Tristan struggled against himself, but he failed. Tears came to his eyes. Quickly, he recovered his composure. He let the rage return, and it was stronger than anything else.

No, he thought. The child hadn't deserved to live. Nor did Martha. The world didn't deserve to exist any longer. The world was just a nightmare that preceded death.

As he left the cathedral and stepped outside, the stars faded into the haze of the new day. The sun's disk emerged red-golden above the rooftops of the cathedral square. He saw a little girl squatting on the cobblestones, holding a Swiss Army knife and examining it closely.

Tristan approached the girl. "Hello, little one!" he said. The girl looked wide-eyed at the man in the long coat who had so suddenly appeared before her.

In passing, Tristan whispered something to her.

Suddenly the girl felt strong. Very strong. In her mind rose promisingly evil ideas of what one could do with a pocket knife.

23

Her opponent was dangerous; she had won every one of her matches so far without effort. Zoe kept a close eye on her. She never seemed to speak a word to her teammates. Nor was she particularly pleased when the first bouts turned out victorious for her team. Individual results in the partial bouts didn't mean too much. Only the overall result counted. Her opponent seemed to have internalized that. It was as if her face was as impenetrable as a fencing mask. She was silent. She was quiet, and Zoe sensed that the saber would speak for this young woman.

This was the junior women's tournament. Each team consisted of three fencers and an unlucky fourth who was only a substitute. The fencing was done in a relay. The first two competitors on each team battled for five points, and the next two took over and continued the fight, until each person had competed.

Many spectators had shown up. They clamored close together on long wooden benches pushed together. The air in the small gymnasium on the outskirts of downtown seemed starved of oxygen. Humidity pressed against one's temples. The gym smelled like sweaty feet, ambition, and loneliness. It stank of the competitors' fear of failure. Of their parents' fear that their daughters were failures. Zoe's parents had never shown up for any of her fights. They hadn't even come when they still thought of themselves as family. Which had been hypocritical even then.

No, Zoe could only rely on one companion. The Senufo saber that Zoe's mother had brought with her from Mali to Germany. The weapon with its awl-shaped blade and short handle made of precious wood had been in her family's possession for generations. As a child, Zoe had marveled at it. It had awakened in her the desire to learn how to fence. It had been an arduous, long journey to fulfill that desire. Against resistance. Against the opposition of her parents, of course. Especially her father, who thought that fencing was not for girls. Also against the resistance of the other children, who teased her.

Are you trying to be white, or what? they taunted. *Why else would someone like you want to dress up in that white fencing outfit?*

The Senufo saber had accompanied her on this long journey. It had given her strength. It was her talisman. Even though it was not regulation and could not be used during fencing training and competitions. But she always took him with her. The Youth Welfare Office, which had otherwise made so many stipulations, had not taken the saber away from Zoe. When the sun sank and she trained alone in the evenings, she used only this saber. She called it Bougeotte. Because in French, *avoir la bougeotte* meant to be restless.

She usually loved her gear. It was a sublime feeling to put it on piece by piece. Pants, stockings, shoes. The undervest and the tight chest protector that was mandatory for women, then a quilted vest. When Zoe put it on, she felt a sensation she never felt elsewhere. The feeling of having value. Of having her own special place in life and of being able to defend it with her own physical strength.

Today, everything was different. The warmth and heaviness of her gear seemed unbearable. Sweat ran between her shoulder blades, collecting at the small of her back. She wished she could tear her fencing gear off.

Zoe's team—TV Freiburg 1844—had won the first round and was now battling it out in the final. The second match had just ended. The opposing team was leading by several points. Zoe was annoyed with her teammates, who were just terrible. But most of all, she was upset with herself. In the relay, Zoe always picked up the final matches. She was by far the best saber fencer on her team. She was known to make up the shortfalls from the partial bouts.

But today, she just didn't have it in her. She had only narrowly won her previous duels against fencers who usually wouldn't have stood a chance against her. She would have to be in top form in the last match against the opponent with the impenetrable face.

But she couldn't focus.

Again and again, the color blue had popped into her mind's eye during the previous match—the blue of the plus sign on the pregnancy test. Again and again, she thought of Fynn. The most disgusting guy who ever existed. The guy she somehow had a crush on. The guy who had gotten her pregnant, because they had been so damned careless. Because he hated condoms, and she hated dutifully swallowing pills that messed with your body. She kept thinking about the little tiny life that was springing up inside her.

She found herself thinking of it with tenderness. That made her furious. She didn't like life. She never had. Life was an imposition. An enemy who constantly harassed you. Who pushed your face into the dirt. Life was nothing but hoarse laughter in the darkness. She had always wanted to extinguish it. So why was she now thinking about that spark of life growing in her belly? She had made a promise to Fynn. She knew that a child would not change his violent resolve. He wouldn't want anything to do with it. He would leave it to die without hesitating: their child and all other living things.

But what if, Zoe thought, she wanted to keep it? If she didn't want it to die? If she wanted it to be born?

The opponents entered the fencing area. Zoe connected herself to the electric scoreboard. The referee checked her weapon by placing a weight on the vertically raised blade tip. He pressed on it, and the hit indicator was triggered. The same thing was done for Zoe's opponent. Everything was working fine. The referee took position next to the piste, the strip on which the opponents would fence. As a further check, the fencers gently struck each other on their electrically conductive jackets, and the hit display was triggered again on both sides. Now Zoe saluted the referee, her opponent, and the spectators and pulled the sweat-soaked mask of fine steel over her face and tightened the neck guard.

The world was now condensed into forty-six-foot length and five-foot width of the piste. Zoe caught sight of her opponent's broad, powerful upper body, which offered a large area for attack. In contrast to épée fencing, only the head, arms, and torso were considered the strike area in saber dueling.

Her pulse pounded in her jaw. She felt the saber bell, a hemisphere around her hand. Tried to get in touch with the weapon, to let it become an extension of her arm. An expression of her will, an expression of her strength. She took up the fencing stance. The command sounded: "Go!"

Zoe's opponent was almost too fast for the eye. She had immediately taken the attack rights, which were necessary for scoring a hit. Zoe was barely able to parry the attack and took too long to counterattack. So another attack came, and then another.

What if, Zoe wondered, *life does matter? What if it does have value? What if I don't want to die after all? Choosing to die voluntarily drag a lot of other people with me may be a big deal, and brave. But isn't it just as brave to choose to stay alive? To face it? To endure it? To defend it? Maybe I will be a mother. Maybe this child will even be able feel to joy. Happiness. Unlike me, who's incapable of it—or refuses it, I don't know. But how am I going to explain this to Fynn? How in the world could I convince him? How can even I convince myself?*

Zoe saw all those faces in front of her again. Children's faces. A whole flood of them, lips moving. She heard one sentence, over and over: *Where can we play?* Suddenly, she felt her strength returning. She fended off another blow, and her lightning-fast riposte landed a hit. Zoe fought her way back into the match. Now it was on. Her teammates called it the Zoe-cane. A hurricane that rode in on a wild horse and trampled her opponent.

Applause filled the hall. Zoe barely noticed. Her glances only brushed the spectators—the hopeful, enthusiastic spectators, all wanting to live. *Live.*

One spectator did not come into Zoe's field of vision. She stood apart in a shadowy corner of the hall. She had been watching Zoe's fight closely. The spectator appeared to be quite young. Early twenties, perhaps. But in truth, she was much older. The spectator wore a dark hooded robe. Only if you looked closely could you see something underneath—a copper glow.

∽

After competitions, Zoe never showered right away. She liked to have the sweat of the fight still clinging to her as she made her way home. Especially if, like today, it was the smell of victory. She didn't yet feel like making her way to the central train station, boarding the wretched train to Kirchzarten, and from there taking the bus to Hofsgrund, which often took forever to arrive. She wanted to stretch her legs a bit. She strolled along the side of the New Town Hall, which was actually a really old building. She walked past the dust-covered basement windows. On a school field trip, she had learned that in the nineteenth century, corpses were delivered to these basement rooms for the then-inadequate study of human anatomy. Where the corpses had come from, no one had wanted to know.

Zoe followed Franciscan Street. She carried her talisman Bougeotte in a slim bag over her shoulder. She walked along one of the Bächle conduits, which was empty of water at the moment, evoking a strange feeling. A feeling of abandonment. She was going to walk over to Kaiser Joseph Avenue, which ran north-south through the center of the city as a main-drag shopping avenue. On this Sunday afternoon, it was surprisingly quiet. Only a hint of fog lay over the dusky city center. But the old colorful houses of Franziskaner Street, which stood in a row like jewelry boxes, seemed to cower as if in anticipation. In anticipation of something evil. The light breeze had died away.

Zoe suddenly felt she had to hurry. Footsteps seemed to follow her. Light footsteps, like a woman's, and firm, somehow unyielding. But when Zoe turned around, there was no one to be seen. The silence was disturbed only by the soft sound of her bag rubbing against her body as she walked.

She was ashamed of her uneasy feeling. *Get a grip,* she told herself. That didn't help much. She tried to concentrate on the fact that she had Bougeotte with her. She would know how to fight back if she needed to.

Zoe reached the historic red Whale House, where the scholar Erasmus of Rotterdam had once lived. She stopped, looked around the modest circular plaza in front of the house that was probably used as a driveway. She saw the large St. Martin's Church, its tall stone back turned to the plaza.

Suddenly she heard his voice. "Was wondering where you were, ace of spades." Fynn stood with leaning against the church wall. She couldn't make out his eyes in the dimness. But she felt their coldness. And she felt something else. She felt a color force its way into her consciousness again—the color blue.

"If you gave a damn about me," she said, "you'd know I had a tournament."

"I knew that," Fynn said. "I wouldn't be here if I didn't. But you don't think I'm going to hold your hand on your little adventures in your fancy white battle outfit."

She took a few hesitant steps toward him. Then something came into her view. The weapon leaning against the church wall beside him: a scythe. It made her shudder.

Zoe remembered a moment once after they had had sex. Most of the time, Fynn was nasty and rough afterward, pushing her away. But just that once, he'd been almost gentle afterward. Compassionate. He'd told her about it. That he owned the scythe his mother had used to murder his father. Zoe hadn't known, back then, if he was just making it all up. Now she saw there must be truth to his story of murder. It fit perfectly with this exciting, uninhibited boy under whose spell she had let herself fall. She had known that he had some dubious accessories. Knives, brass knuckles. That he had his strange whims. Enigmatic tendencies enhanced the attraction. But keeping a murder weapon like a relic was downright creepy to her.

"I have to go," she said. He cut her off, grabbing the scythe at the same time. He held it like a walking stick. The flashing curve of blade grinned in her face.

"You don't think I'm just going to let you go," he said. "It's time. Come with me. He's expecting us."

"Who?"

"You know who I'm talking about. Tristan Nightsworn. I know you've seen him, too, in your dreams. He has something to show us. The two of us won't be alone in this."

"That's right," Zoe said. "We won't be alone. There'll be a baby. Ours. If we let it. If we let it have a life." After a brief pause, she continued, "Have you ever had any doubts, Fynn? Did you ever think that what we promised ourselves was wrong? That death might not be the answer? You saw it yourself when you were a little boy. You should know."

Fynn's face showed no emotion. But Zoe sensed something stirring inside him.

"Are you dumping me?" he asked in a quiet voice. "Abandoning me? Are you planning to betray me?"

"This is not betraying," Zoe said. "I want to free you. Free us."

His fist hit her in the face so hard and abruptly that she slumped to the ground. Blood poured from her nose. Then she felt the cold scythe blade against her neck and heard Fynn's voice: "Either you're with me, or you're my enemy. If you choose the wrong path, I won't spare you. So don't be surprised if I hand you your own head."

The coldness of the scythe blade receded. Zoe rose with difficulty. She heard a voice from deep within the shadows cast by the great church across the street.

"Well said, Fynn. May I take over?"

Something detached from the shadows. A face. A body. The man she knew from her dream—the man who had emerged from the gloom of Lake Flint and whom Fynn called Tristan Nightsworn. The stranger approached her.

He held a curved sword in his right hand, with a bluish shining blade. Zoe knew at once that he was the one who had killed Isabel and the others. She had no doubt about it. This man named Tristan Nightsworn was a monster. And Fynn had allied himself with him.

Quick as a flash, Zoe pulled her Senufo saber from her pack and tried to attack. She knew how crucial a quick strike was. But he was so agile that his movements were almost a blur to her. Their blades clashed a few times, and she realized she was no match for him. In a last burst of strength, she aimed for his head. But the blade whistled just over the top of his skull. Then the man effortlessly knocked the saber out of her hand.

Before she knew it, she was once again lying on the hard cobblestones. He was above her. She wanted to scream, but he squeezed her mouth shut. Finally, she saw his face, a beautiful face and at the same time the cruelest face she had ever seen. Zoe the evil in the darkness of an infinite depth of emptiness in his eyes.

"I know what's in your belly," he whispered in her ear. "I know your secret. I'm going to cut it out of you. Let's find out how much pain you can endure."

With the blade of his sword, he slowly cut open her clothes. First the coat, then the sweatshirt. She tried to fight back, clawing her fingernails into his back, slashing at him, to no avail. She was helpless. As if bound in a strait-jacket. As if forced into a vise.

Zoe felt a draft of air as a figure in a dark hooded robe landed, crouching, beside them. The man looked up. Then everything happened incredibly fast.

The figure rose, the hood fell back to reveal a woman with curly hair. She drew a sword from her robe. The blade hissed through the air and bit into his shoulder. Zoe was covered in a spray of the man's blood. The man staggered to one side, his face contorted in pain, and the woman pulled Zoe up as Fynn swept the scythe blade on them both with a mighty swing. The woman spun and fended off the blow and punched him in the face, sending him tumbling backward to the ground. She hurled the scythe away through the air in a high arc, and it landed on the cobblestones with a clatter. Then the woman moved toward Tristan Nightsworn, who was still crouched on the ground. She tried to bring her blade down on his chest, he yanked up his own sword. The blades clashed against each other. Sparks flew out. Zoe had to close her eyes. When she opened them again, the two were facing each other but not moving. They looked at each other in silence. Infinite anger was in their gazes, and something else: sadness. The tips of their blades were pointed at each other's chest. Both could have stabbed at any moment. But they did not. Then the man smiled.

"You know the rules," he said. "They are anchored to our hearts. The first eight days have passed. You can't kill me anymore than I can kill you. Only when the Called Ones have been determined. In the last battle. But it is not yet time for the end."

"Get away from me!" the woman shouted. Zoe saw that there were tears in her eyes now. "Get away and take your odious minion with you! We will meet again!"

"Yes, we will, my dear," Tristan Nightsworn replied. Again, Zoe was struck by his cruelly handsome face. Attractive in a relentless way. In the same way as Fynn.

Glancing at Zoe, he added, "I like her. Don't let her slip through your fingers!" Then he pulled Fynn, who had regained his feet, along with him, and they disappeared down an alley between two houses.

⤬

Zoe picked Bougeotte up from the ground. She didn't understand what just had happened. Her eyes blurred with tears. She hated to cry, because tears were a sign of weakness and because every tear shed in the world was, in her opinion, in vain. Anger rose in her to fill the space. The woman approached her. Wanted to stroke her face with a hand to comfort her. Zoe pushed her back.

"I don't need your help," she hissed. "I'll be fine on my own. I could have handled the whole thing just fine without you. Who are you, anyway? Why did you barge in?" On a sudden impulse, she struck out at the woman with Bougeotte. The woman parried the blow with ease. She cleverly took advantage of the moment after the strike when Zoe was off balance balance. A light push was enough, and Zoe fell to the ground. Again.

"My name is Martha," the woman said, helping her up. "I know your name is Zoe. I know a lot about you. I imagine that it would do you good if you let someone help you from time to time. Being helped creates a sense of connection. Maybe then you'd feel less lonely, less powerless."

"What's that supposed to be?" Zoe said. "A life lesson?"

"No, a reminder. We need the help of others. And now we need it even more. More than ever. Not just you, but all of humanity. You have experienced this man's power firsthand. You've seen him in your dreams. You know what will happen if no one stops him."

"Why do you think I want to stop him?"

"I can't be sure you do."

"I thought you knew so much about me? Seems like there are some gaps in your knowledge after all."

"Yes," Martha said. "The gap in knowledge is called the future. I can only trust that you want to stop him, too. That the love in you will prevail. That you will choose to fight. Against him. Against his allies. Against the destruction they want to cause. I can only trust that you will join us."

"Us?"

"Our little band."

"What are you talking about?"

Martha smiled. "A small band that's trying to save the world."

Zoe stared at Martha. In that moment, she felt it—that life was a home. A home that no one wanted to be driven from. Not even her.

"Okay," Zoe said. "I'll check out your stupid squad."

24

Mistilo was grand. Mistilo was powerful. And he craved blood.

He was up high, on the pyramidal roof of the Swabian Gate. He crouched under a verdigris-strewn roof lantern that remotely resembled a tied-up coin bag.

Mistilo let his gaze wander. People suspected nothing. Not yet. It was early morning. Freezing cold. The sun rose ponderously over the rooftops.

That man had also suspected nothing. The policeman, who loved girls and only the day before had harassed some young thing again. For a few days now, it was like nothing was holding him back. Ever since that mysteriously attractive man had invaded the gun store, he had changed. He had become even more rampant. No longer had any inhibitions. He had warned the girl in no uncertain terms about what he would do to her if she refused to fulfill his desires. After all, he could have his nasty revenge on her entire family—her mother, father, everyone. He was a policeman, and always had the upper hand.

Tristan Nightsworn had given Mistilo a mission. Mistilo would fulfill it. Mistilo was unstoppable. He was furiously fast. He was ruthless. He was not bound by normal pathways. He could climb over the rooftops.

Mistilo looked in the direction of the old townhouses.

It was quiet on the streets and alleys. He saw the Oberlinden fountain. Saw the Red Bear inn. He had the policeman in his sights. The policeman was on the road again this morning, not on duty. He was not in uniform. No pistol. His weapon of choice was something else today. And he planned to use it.

Mistilo followed the man, leaping almost silently from rooftop to rooftop. The man strolled over the cobblestones of the sprawling, slightly sloping Augustinian Square, where people always boozed and bawled in the evenings.

Three schoolgirls had stopped there on their way to school. The policeman had arranged to meet them. More precisely, he had ordered them to come.

He had no idea that Mistilo would come.

The square was empty except for the three girls. It was quick. They would never forget it. The brief rain of blood. The beast that had appeared out of nowhere and pounced on the policeman, slashed himm and carried him away in its claws.

25

Where do I find the love to let go of your hand?

She waited. Her eyes searched the rooftops and the sky. Lost in the tangle of paths, lost in small alleys. She waited for the magpie.

She had promised. Her friend, her love, just before she died. She would return as the creature whose name she had taken. She had been the magpie, and Kathryn was the crow. They flew together through the heights of life and down into deep chasms. They belonged to each other. They were free. But then something caught them. Invisible, taking its time. It knew its power. Knew it would win. It was called leukemia. It froze her smile, broke her wings. And then there was nothing but the vast emptiness of the air.

But the magpie would return. Nothing to hinder her flight. They would be together again. But it was not yet time. Her love did not come. And still did not come.

Kathryn waited.

⌒

The magpie, whose real name was Rebecca, had also waited long enough. For a full twelve months, during which Kathryn was no longer really responsive. For four of those months—while autumn took over from summer—she had worked through the community service hours imposed on her, in the St. Marienhaus psychiatric ward on Tal Street.

It was a halfway tolerable atmosphere. But her heart beat as if in an already dead body. She had not been capable of much. She passed the time almost exclusively in the dull, musty rooms of the psychiatric ward for adolescents, while the days rolled by like shadows outside the windows, and the door to the wardroom opened, closed, and reopened, and a voice dulled by habit called across the corridors, "Medication time!"

What had led to those stumbling months was a night in July.

A night she would never forget.

It had been unbearably humid. Not a breath of wind stirred. Her clothes stuck to her skin. The sky had a hardness that was spreading to the people beneath it.

Rebecca and Kathryn had just come from Pi, a club where mostly students hung out. They were actually too young to be let in there. But they both looked like they were well over eighteen. They'd never had any problem getting in.

Kathryn clearly remembered the shifting mood of the party that night. She and Rebecca had argued violently, then made out violently, then argued again. They had been drunk, of course. Not very, but enough. As they emerged from the club, streetlamps gleamed on the cobblestones. A little later, blood would gleam there. A couple of teenagers had shown up. Insulted them.

Dirty lesbians! Don't you wanna try a dick? You don't know what you're missing!

They tagged along next to Rebecca and Kathryn, not letting themselves be shaken off. One of them loomed closer and closer. Kathryn often still saw him in her dreams. Saw his short hair. The small scar on his face that looked like a thumbnail.

Almost, nothing happened. Almost.

But when the guy had groped Kathryn, she had popped open the jackknife she always carried. She stabbed the guy. Then came the blood. Lots of it. Too much. She had almost killed the guy. Almost.

She'd heard muffled screams and Rebecca's voice calling "Crow!" over and over again, as if she was actually trying to summon the spirit of a sinister bird. Mist rose before Kathryn's eyes. When it dissipated, Kathryn felt like she had passed into another world. A world in which color no longer existed. The flickering blue light of the police car had long been her last experience of color. After that, their world had sunk into black-and-white. Magpies' plumage was black-and-white. That should have given her hope. But hope had faded like any other colors. Only sometimes, when Rebecca had visited her in the psychiatric ward, would Kathryn see the blue glow of a magpie's wings in her dream afterward.

⸎

Crow hadn't stolen anything in a long time. It wasn't that her sense of morality had changed after everything that had happened to her. But she just didn't feel like stealing as often anymore. She had grown tired. Tired of her heart. She had never stolen to get big money, anyway. She didn't want to drain accounts and put people in financial trouble. She had always sent the credit cards she found in the wallets back to the banks in envelopes with no return address. She had also sent the ID cards to the owners, since their addresses were right there on them. For her, stealing was more of an adventure and, at the same time, a kind of relaxation. It made her feel like a being from another sphere who could sneak into other people's daily lives unnoticed. She loved to get in touch with strangers in this particular way and to uncover little bits of their world, tiny pieces of their dreams. And if, in addition, some cash came her way, so much the better.

True, she hadn't stolen in a long time. But that day, she felt the urge to do it again. The morning hours were good for it. When the Münster Market, with its colorful stalls, attracted people's attention. She knew that her decision was dangerous. During her months in the clinic, she had behaved exceptionally well, and the oh-so-well-behaved society had now slowly embraced her again. Crow would be rushing back into a massive pile of shit if she was caught stealing. But a sense of futility had settled over her today. She needed something to bring her something close to happiness. However fleeting it might be. She didn't know if she would be as adept at it as she had been in the past. Mainly because she had lost her eye for color. Stealing required not only skill and precise timing but also a good eye.

She did not admit it to herself, but something in her even wished that she would get caught.

She had the morning off. She was not expected at the blacksmith's shop, where she had been working for several weeks now, until late in the afternoon. The workshop belonged to a woman in her fifties whose hands almost seemed to match the hardness of the material they were dealing with. But the loud pounding of the hundred-year-old spring hammers had not deafened her to the nuances of life. She looked after Kathryn with great benevolence. She entrusted her with a variety of smaller jobs. Kathryn especially excelled at making the *schepsers*, which forest workers used to peel the bark from tree trunks. Kathryn liked dipping the schepsers into the hardening oil after the initial sharpening and to see the flames emerge, though she saw the colors only in her memory.

Kathryn liked this workshop. Liked the blacksmith, although she was not at all comfortable with that. She felt she didn't deserve the woman's warmth. That's why she smashed that cordiality with resentment.

Later, Crow zoomed down Kaiser Joseph Avenue on her skateboard. She had spent a beautiful morning in the hustle and bustle of people. The odds had been good. She realized she was still as skilled as ever. Had gotten herself some cash. She was pleased with herself. Jolly, even.

Then she dug the key out of her pocket. A special key. Inconspicuous. Burnished by time. Her talisman.

A few years ago, she had managed to steal this very lucky key from a man who was head of municipal building management. The key fitted into an unusual door that provided access to a Freiburg landmark—the key to get inside the Martin Gate. Sixty meters high, with its Gothic-looking roof and four corner towers, the gate had once been part of the city wall. Today it was a passageway for the streetcars. Hardly anyone saw the Martin Gate from the inside. Some birds knew it. It had been her secret hiding place. The key had led Crow and Magpie there many a time. Their lips had found each other, within the dark protection of the stone walls in the middle of the bustling city center.

Crow had not been here in a very long time. But today, she felt like it. The key still fit.

The mysterious-looking iron door with its heavy grate opened. A musty smell rose to her nose as she climbed the narrow spiral staircase. She used her phone as a flashlight. It was so dark that she wouldn't have been able to see otherwise. The light fell on cobwebs that clung to the walls and steps. It was evident that no one had been here for a long time. She was startled when she almost stepped on a small furry body on one step—a dead rat. The stairs, just like the small decomposing body, were speckled with dots. Crow did not see their colors, but she was sure they were confetti from the last carnival parade.

Crow climbed higher and higher, until the stone staircase ended and she reached the gatehouse structure, a platform of about ten by eleven yards. She leaned the skateboard against a wall and crouched down on the floor. She thought back to that day in midsummer when she had been here with Rebecca. Her team had played a game that same day. Back then, they had both played soccer. A time that seemed infinitely far in the past for Kathryn, even though only a few years had passed since then. Kathryn's folding knife had been used mainly for carving. The blade had not yet come into contact with blood. And Rebecca's illness had still been asleep, though one eye of the disease had already opened a crack. No one had noticed. Not even Rebecca herself.

Yes, Kathryn still remembered that day well. The B youth team of SC Freiburg had won 2–1 against the favorites from FFC Frankfurt. Kathryn, coming from the left wing, had hit a high cross inside, and Rebecca had headed in the winning goal. A perfect day. Not long after the game, they had come here to The Martin Gate. Crow remembered how the darkness had descended upon them and how she had embraced the heat of her desire.

Kathryn climbed narrow wooden stairs from one false ceiling to the next, just as she had done with Rebecca. Her fingers slid along the dust-covered handrail of the stairs. Rebecca had told Kathryn that there had been a dungeon in the Martin Gate tower several centuries before. It was said that the men and women who were imprisoned there had been given St. Martin's cloaks. Crow thought about the fact that she, too, now wore this coat. On her way up, she ignored the yellow sign warning that the floor had been treated with rat poison years ago. One of the reasons why the inside of the gate was empty. She reached the room where the old clockwork was located, where the bells dangled from the heavy wooden ceiling beams. Then she pushed open the door to the perimeter battlements and found herself out in the open, above the city.

Almost none of the noise of the busy traffic and shopping thoroughfare could be heard from up there. Not even a slight vibration could be felt when a streetcar passed through the gate. Kathryn sucked in the fresh air. She saw the curved line of Kaiser Joseph Avenue, the Munster Tower.

She let her gaze glide over rooftops.

Suddenly she saw it, a creature crouching not far from her on one of the rooftops. At first, she thought that it must be a big black animal. But then she quickly realized: what she saw there was not an animal at all. It was a creature such as one would encounter only in nightmares. Crow's breath stopped for a moment. She felt a weakness in her knees. She felt the blood drain from her face. And the soles of her feet went ice-cold in her sneakers. The beast held a lifeless body its clawed hands. With horror, Kathryn saw that it was a human body. That of a man. It seemed as if it had struck its prey and dragged it away—up to the roof. Probably to devour it there. Crow still did not perceive any colors, but she noticed very clearly that its eyes were glowing when the beast looked up. She saw the nostrils moving rhythmically, saw the maw of the mouth opening to reveal enormous teeth. Kathryn even had the feeling that she could smell this creature, a smell like a swamp. And in her mouth, she suddenly had a taste of cinnamon and blood. Finally the beast seemed to notice her. For a few horrifyingly long seconds, it stared across at Kathryn.

There was a hissing sound, and for a moment, Kathryn heard a gurgling voice, and she thought she could make out one word: *Mistilo*.

In a heartbeat, a tremendous weight landed on her, knocking the breath out of her. She was thrown back into the room where the bells hung. Kathryn lay sprawled on the floor. Claws dug into her flesh. Then she saw nothing but the horrible face of this beast and the smoldering gaze of its eyes.

The slavering teeth came closer. The jaws closed around the arm Kathryn had yanked up to protect her throat. Her body reared up under the creature's force. She could feel her strength fading. She wanted to scream, but only a dry rattle came from her throat.

Suddenly her senses caught something—the breeze of a flapping wing. Kathryn's eyes managed to escape the beast's gaze for a scant second, and she saw the bird. The magpie flew up and landed next to her on the wooden floor. For a few seconds that seemed detached from time, there was nothing else for Kathryn but the beautiful bird that had appeared out of nowhere. The magpie looked at her sideways with one black eye. Black with sensation. Black with memory.

Her head swirled with words she thought she had long forgotten. The lines of a poem she had written shortly before Rebecca died. She had never read it to her because she had been ashamed of it and, what's more, afraid of bursting into tears.

Where do I find the love to let go of your hand?
How do I let you go into the uncertain hour
Knowing that it strikes only for you
And I can do nothing to protect you?
From where will come that love?

The magpie was still watching Kathryn. From out of the sadness that had overcome Kathryn, a new feeling suddenly emerged. A warmth that flowed directly to her heart. She felt her strength returning. Now she knew that she would never lose Rebecca.

The magpie's body seemed to evaporate, become invisible. Beside her now on the wooden floor lay a long dagger that looked like a great wing feather. Still resisting the beast's attack, Kathryn managed to grab the dagger. She rammed the blade into its body.

The giant gaping mouth contorted in pain, and Kathryn was released, flung to the side. As she sat up, leaning on one hand, she saw a slimy fluid run from the beast's wound. It seemed unfazed by this, however, not weakened at all. The creature glared at Kathryn with its glowing eyes. At any moment, she expected another attack. It lowered its head almost to the ground, as if it wanted to absorb her scent deeply like a bloodhound. Then its horrible head swung back. The creature turned around and jumped out and away with a mighty leap. Kathryn quickly followed it outside. She saw it hurry across the rooftops until it arrived back at the man's lifeless body. There it turned again to look at Kathryn. Again she heard the gurgling voice: *Mistilo knows. Soon you will be only a cold corpse. Soon!* Then the beast ran with its prey from roof to roof and seemed to shrink until it was no bigger than a child, a dancing flame, and then just a dark glimmer in the distance.

Kathryn stared after it, aghast. She stared at the rooftops of the city, which lay colorlessly spread out before her. Her tension gradually faded, but her heart was still racing. Her right hand still grasped the handle of the long dagger, which was like a blood-stained bird's feather. She was breathing fast, breathing the cool air. Suddenly the sun, a flow of white, seemed to point at something as if with a finger. And suddenly, Kathryn saw it. Faintly at first, then more pronounced. Stronger. It was moving down there in the hustle and bustle of people. It stood out. What caught Kathryn's eye for the very first time in many months was color. Not black, not white. But metal: copper. The color emanated from a person walking along down there. When she looked closer, she recognized someone she had known once. A young man who was the same age as she was. She had once been in a class with him. His name was Daniel. She had liked him. Had often defended him because, as an underdog, he was sort of begging to be beaten up. Strictly speaking, she hadn't liked him because of that, but because he had something in him that was denied to her. Faith. Faith in a higher power. Faith in goodness. Kathryn had envied Daniel for that.

She realized this now when she saw the copper color that emanated from him. Daniel was walking toward the Martin Gate. And then she noticed that this color came from something he was carrying. A sword. Instinctively, she sensed that he was here for her. That he needed her. As he had needed her then. And that she needed him to awaken it in her, again and again: faith.

Suddenly she could reconcile everything in her mind: The ghastly creature and the dagger. The magpie, her magpie who had returned, and the young man whose name was Daniel. Now she saw how he looked up at her. And she watched as the black-and-white receded entirely. Saw how the first dots appeared like in an oil painting and how a whole world emerged from these dots. A world that was filled with colors.

26

Tristan Nightsworn was standing on the southern shore of Lake Flint. He had collected dried marigolds in the forest to treat the wound on his shoulder. True, he had found only a few, and in autumn, they somewhat lacked in vigor. Still, they did him good, and he felt the healing slowly beginning.

The sky was pearly gray. At least where the dense coniferous trees gave a clear view. Their damp branches were teeming with starlings, which swooped up again and again. This filled the forest with a steady murmur as if water were flowing through a pipe. Otherwise, it was tranquil. Tiny waves nipped against the shore.

At Tristan's side was the beast Mistilo. It, too, had been wounded. But that injury was no match for the dark power that filled this creature. The important thing: Mistilo had fulfilled his mission. He had made the sacrifice—the corpse of the policeman.

Then came the other two. Just as he had expected them to. Tristan had never doubted that they would appear.

The two of them stepped out from between the tall spruce trees: Fynn, who had pulled the hood of his hoodie over his head, and Henry B. Lindt, the gaze of his cold, determined eyes fixed on Tristan and Mistilo. Fynn and Henry carried their weapons, scythe and rapier.

Tristan pointed to the corpse at his feet with a solemn gesture.

"Dinner is served. Our ritual can begin. Now, do as I command and let the flesh disappear into your maw. Just as all living things sooner or later disappear into the maw of death. Through this meal, the power of death will awaken in you. Its greed, which cannot be tamed. And you will experience the joy of this greed." He gazed at his companions. He smiled when he saw how unafraid the three of them were. He smiled when he saw that they did not hesitate for a moment.

27

Tristan Nightsworn had been right. The meal was delicious. Gnawing on a knuckle, Henry B. Lindt remembered the times when he had been a boy and he had sat alone in the magnificent dining room of the villa, on a chair on which his petite body was almost lost. The chair was a symbol of the great jeweled world in which he could go about his mischief unmolested, like a castle ghost. His father was rarely at home.

He remembered how he had loved it when his tongue came in contact with the fat of the meat in his goulash. That little bit of fat had meant everything to the boy. In a way, it had given him a taste of the intense pleasures that awaited him in abundance outside of the mansion. Not the least of which was the joy of violence, in which some poor devil always came to evil harm. It wouldn't be him. He had made sure of that.

He was high with a kind of intoxication. He felt power awakening in him. Nothing could compare.

After a while, he heard Tristan's voice: "I am proud of you. I know that you are ready now. The second part of our ritual awaits you. Follow me!" Tristan waded slowly into Lake Flint in his cloak. Mistilo, the gruesome beast, immediately obeyed his command. The young fellow named Fynn also put aside his scythe and started moving.

For a few seconds, Henry was overcome with doubt. Was it really right to hand himself over entirely to this man Tristan Nightsworn? But then he thought about the joy of his intoxication, the ecstasy of this community. People—beings—joining together. All of them filled with the same darkness. A darkness that would soon be unleashed.

Henry thought of the joy that came with the doom. The pleasure that Tristan could bring to him. Only him. No one else.

He jammed his rapier into the damp earth and followed the others. Waded into the water, on and on. Not knowing what awaited him.

The mirror of the lake begin to ripple quietly, though not a breath of wind stirred. The ripples grew stronger until small quarrelsome waves grew into a wild lashing out of the water on all sides. He saw Tristan dive below the surface. The others followed him. Henry, too, followed him.

Fluid coldness surrounded him. Briefly, he saw Mistilo darting down into the depths like a giant predatory fish. His senses began to fade. He didn't know where he was or where the others were. Didn't know who he was anymore. Henry felt a sucking current pulling him down into the abyss. It lasted until his name came back to him. Until he could feel his own body again. He had closed his eyes, pressed his lips together. Suppressed with all his might the impulse to breathe. When he carefully opened his eyes, he saw them, at first blurred, but then in strange clarity. They approached him from all sides—mixed-up creatures. The lower half of their bodies reminded him of the dark slithering bodies of moray eels, but out of that emerged the humanlike torsos of picture-perfect women. He saw their hair, which seemed soft and flowing like water itself. He saw their magnificent breasts. The creatures breathed their breath into him. He felt this breath permeating him, taking over all areas of his body. Never before had his lungs been filled with such sweetness.

The creatures disappeared again. The current pulled him down farther and farther. The waters swirled around him in the depths. Ghastly creatures emerged from the eddies. Newts, mollusks, giant jellyfish, sea spiders, water snakes, and other vermin swarmed around him. Among them, grimacing faces appeared, staring at him from their distorted features. The apparitions seemed to lust after him, but he escaped them in the current that was pulling him still, farther and farther down.

All at once, there was no more movement. The water was now still and dark, but his eyes still saw with that unnatural clarity. Below him, he saw a wall—the walls of a sunken fortress. Then suddenly there was no more water but instead air smelling of rot, which he greedily gulped as he plunged down a black, stony abyss.

The walls raced past him. He landed on a hard stone floor that seemed to ram his legs into his body, forcing the air out of his lungs. As he rose in intense pain, he saw that he was in a windowless hall where water dripped from the high walls and ran across a floor covered with slimy growths. Otherwise, there was little to indicate that this was the bottom of a lake. There was air to breathe, and this could have just as easily been the inside of an ancient castle deep in the woods. At the front of the hall, Tristan sat on a stone seat that looked like a weathered throne.

"Do you like it?" Tristan asked, his voice echoing off the walls. When Henry looked around, he saw that Mistilo and Fynn had made it this far, too.

Tristan, his hair dripping, rose and took the three of them into his gaze. His eyes seemed to light up as he said, "Thisplace is Xanas, the dark fortress after which my sword is named. This fortress will be the place where you will come to know my sword. To learn what it means to fight. And here you will know, also, the horror of it."

28

S uddenly he saw it, the rectangular opening where the descending staircase ended. The opening looked like a gate into nothingness. Nothing was visible beyond it.

It was about six feet high and three wide. Simple, unadorned. There was nothing threatening about it. Nevertheless, Fynn, whose wet clothes stuck to his skin, suddenly felt sick to his stomach, like something was tugging at his guts. This portal, enclosed in a narrow frame, seemed to mark the end . . . the end of all things.

All at once the intoxicating joy of before was extinguished. Tristan Nightsworn had led them through the main hall of the Xanas fortress at the bottom of the lake, through rooms that looked like dark grottos, until they came to the very narrow, very gloomy staircase.

"Who wants to be first?" asked Tristan. He looked questioningly at Mistilo, glanced at Fynn, and then at Henry.

"What is that structure?" Henry asked, his eyes fixed on the portal.

A malicious smile crossed Tristan's face.

"This is where your path leads. When you pass through this opening, you will experience the horror of humanity. It will enter your souls. You will experience images of violence, despair, and destruction. Until you become one with them. Until your path will be the horror and the horror your path. You're not hesitating, are you?"

Henry did not meet Tristan's gaze. He started to move forward. Fynn watched the color drain from his face as he slowly descended the stairs and approached the opening. He put one foot in and disappeared. With a short, feverish breath, Fynn sucked in the air that smelled of ammonia and seaweed. He strained to listen but heard nothing. There was only silence, which was becoming a palpable pressure on his eardrums. His eyes strained at the enigmatic rectangle at the foot of the stairs. He didn't know how much time passed.

When Henry returned, he had changed. His hair had gone pure white, and he wore a coat similar to Tristan's. His eyes were hard and shimmering like blue zircons.

Next, it was Mistilo's turn. Tristan Nightsworn nodded at him. Snorting, Mistilo took a leap, and the rectangle swallowed the beast. It did not return. What returned was a young man Fynn knew from school. His name was Balder. He, too, wore a coat, and in his eyes was a deep cold blue. In his right hand, he held a double-edged longsword as black as volcanic glass. Fynn sensed that the creature Mistilo, his mighty power, darkness, and bloodlust, had been absorbed into this sword.

Tristan gave Fynn a prompting look.

Slowly he descended the stairs, approached the opening.

So now the time has come, he thought. *Now all the boundaries will be blown sky high.* Now his whole being would become an instrument directed toward a single goal: annihilation.

But suddenly, images surfaced in him that had long been submerged. Images that were accompanied by a feeling of happiness. Images of beauty that countered the gloom of death. Images of life.

He felt transported back to the time when he had been a boy. He saw his mother, then still with a radiant smile. He saw how she helped him feed an injured pigeon for which he had built a small sickbed on the terrace. He saw how cheerfully his mother met him when he came racing down the driveway in his go-cart. And then he saw Zoe and realized for the first time how fond he was of her. Her expressive, unusual voice. Her untamed hair. The spicy aroma of her skin. He thought of how intense it was when they had sex.

He looked at the rectangle, knew what it would mean if he went in there. He made his decision. He pushed down the images of life, the images of beauty. Zoe was nothing, worth nothing. She was a foreign bitch, nothing more. And life was just a pile of shit. He took a step, and the rectangle swallowed his body. Devoured his mind.

29

Martha sat alone on one of the benches in the small chapel. Her eyes were closed. She felt the need to pray. To pray as she used to, all the time. But she had been foolish then. She had not known. Not known that no prayer in the world had ever pushed back the violence. All it took was a spark in the withered landscapes of the soul, and a fire was kindled that spread on and on.

As she traced her thoughts, she felt her fingers tighten around the grip of her sword. Her eyelids lifted. The light of day seeped through the stained-glass windows, cascading colors across her face. Summoning the colors of her past. With her eyes open, she dreamed—dreams of remembrance.

With the end of her existence before her, Martha tried to shoo away old images and gather her thoughts, but they led her to the wildly kicking life in her womb. The old life tried to break through forcefully, right there and then, just as her new life was about to come to an abrupt end. Images and fragments of thoughts from that time drew near . . .

Martha would have held her protecting hands in front of her belly if she could. With tender circling movements, she would try to calm her child, which was moving wildly in her womb. As if it knew what was about to happen. The birth was imminent, and there had been a contraction or two over the past two days. Martha had hoped that it could be born soon. She had hoped to be able to save it. Since she had been discovered a few days earlier in St. Margaret's and had been pushed down into the chapel crypt like a criminal and locked up there, she had been given only a few sips of water, and neither a blanket nor a meal. She had crouched down on the stone floor between two sarcophagi, absorbed in the movements of the child in her belly so as not to be overcome by her horrible fear. Then they had dragged her out of the dungeon and tied her arms and legs to a stake in the clearing.

Brushwood and logs were piled up under her bare feet so that in some places, sharp splinters of wood pierced her skin.

Martha had looked into the eyes of death so many times before and had determined to go bravely into this final battle. Only her failure to protect the child broke her heart. The child that was Tristan Nightsworn's. She had resolved to embrace it with her love until her last breath, to stand by it and not to be distracted from it for anything in the world. But now, she could do nothing to help it. She looked up.

Gathered in a circle around the pyre were peasants in their drab gray-brown robes, women in aprons and dirty white caps, children barefoot in rags, and all sorts of riff-raff from the surrounding area. Even the odd warrior from the lower nobility. All wanted to witness the rare spectacle at close quarters.

Martha skimmed the rows of spectators, and her gaze lingered on the side entrance to the chapel. There in the background, far behind the last row of onlookers, under the protection of the chapel's eaves, stood his impressive figure.

He towered over all the others in height, his turquoise Egyptian cloak standing out in colorful splendor. Martha hated the weakness that was about to bring her body to its knees. She withstood his cold, merciless gaze that pierced her as if he could use it to light the flames of the pyre even now.

Tristan Nightsworn had betrayed her, and now he had come to watch his child die.

She had loved him, this irresistible warrior, the crusader with whom she had fought side by side, who had led her from her lowly life as a Black Forest peasant girl into the world of nobility and knighthood. They had been comrades-in-arms by day and lovers by night.

In the winter of 1218, Martha and Tristan had been drawn into the turmoil of the Fifth Crusade. She had fled her poor home village that did not even have a name, just a collection of puny huts. She had fled on a December night with pallid light as if the night held back its darkness to deny Martha any protection. Yet, she had managed to escape. She had left behind her sister Keth and her sick mother, whom she had loved so dearly. With terrible remorse, but with the hope of young exuberance for an independent life and to leave poverty and despair behind. She had posed as a squire and had advanced unrecognized to the upper ranks of knighthood.

It was the winter when the Crusaders were trying to take Egypt and from there begin the reconquest of Jerusalem, which they had lost years before and which Pope

Innocent III had so fervently identified as the center of Christianity.

Tristan had always been at her side. He had an attraction that Martha had found difficult to resist. His irrepressible strength, the beauty and elegance of his appearance, and his nobility had given him a grandeur that Martha, disguised as a man, had been unable to resist. With him, for the first time, she had felt so alive, as if unearthly powers flowed through her veins. Tristan had recognized the shine in her eyes; many ladies before her had fallen at his feet.

He had seen through her secret early on, but had left her in suspense, had ridden with her into battles and left the ground covered with the dead. He had slept side by side with her in the mud under the stars. He had never tired of explaining to her, secretly and with beautiful words, what a brave fighter and attractive woman was in that iron armor.

During the day, they would fight together under the scorching sun, and at night they would make passionate love. Sometimes, when attack was imminent, and they held out in the dark of night to surprise the enemy forces, he would quietly tell her about his family.

He would tell her about the ancient lineage of his ancestors, who had all been warriors, just like him. He would tell her about the sunken fortress of Xanas, which his family had inhabited for many centuries. One day he would take her there, would show her the place where it had been submerged in a flood that had burst from the rocks.

But Martha had waited for that day in vain. Over the course of three years of fighting, Tristan had begun to change. The exhilaration that had carried him through the battles, that had given him an invisible shield and had made him almost invulnerable, had started to change. He had stopped fighting for Bishop Olivier, who had won over so many knights with his speeches. Tristan had stopped fighting for the pope and his ideas and certainly had stopped fighting for God. He had fought only to kill. He had begun to take on paid duels away from the battlefields for less courageous companions. He had himself hired for minor, distant skirmishes. And after the lost crusade, he had hired himself out as a mercenary to meddle in any war that would have him, with Martha at his side. The irrepressible power within him had increasingly become hatred and violence.

The sublime and upright nobleman had turned into a haughty and condescending being, merciless and brutal with his opponents, imperious and aggressive with Martha.

Godfearing Martha had been terrified by the mere slaughter, fight for the fight's sake. She had held her faith in God and in their truth, in the Holy Land, which had to be brought back into the hands of Christianity.

With every exchange of words they had about his change, Tristan had become more aggressive, insulting and beating her.

Sometimes, in the rare bright moments of the day, he would explain to her that this restlessness, this irrepressible will to fight, was an indomitable part of him. A bloodlust, passed down from his ancient lineage, from generation to generation, deep in his guts. All his ancestors supposedly had this viciousness and baseness in them.

Then he would again fall into a gloom and coldness that made Martha tremble.

Had God sent her this man so that she would deliver him from this madness? She had wondered this during the long frosty nights without sleep, before the cruel battles, while she watched Tristan pacing up and down their tent-like a wild animal.

Could God possibly embrace such a creature, even forgive him? Perhaps with God's help, she would be able to convert Tristan, she had thought. But at the same time, she had known that her willpower would not be enough to stand against him, that the maelstrom of violence would pull her with him into the darkness that surrounded him.

Could she have continued to love him as she did? Would that love have given her the strength to stay with him? Martha waged a hopeless battle with herself. She had wrestled with her love for him, with her revulsion, with her pity, and with her rage, which would come over her most violently when he took her rough and hard on the bare earth of her lodgings.

After one of those nights, when her whole body had felt sore and ravaged, Martha had known that she could stay no longer. No army in the world could rid Tristan of his cruelty.

When they had joined a mercenary army in Anatolia that had been engaged in skirmishes around Constantinople for months, Martha had made her plan.

The leaders' meeting was her only chance. Before impending defeats and difficult battles, the key men would meet to discuss strategy and tactics. But, most of the time, these meetings would degenerate into drunken binges that lasted well into the night. They would help themselves to local whores and sleep it off on the spot. Thus, Martha would have a head start of almost a day for her escape. Moreover, she had been sure that Tristan would not run away from an important battle to look for her. He would lose prestige and jeopardize his standing. And he would never have let that happen.

Packing a few belongings and the last of her food from the night before, she had slipped into the paddock and saddled her horse for a long, harrowing ride, back to where she had come from long ago. She would save the child she had been carrying in her womb for a few weeks. She would brave the long ride that would take her back home.

But Martha had known Tristan would come looking for her, sooner or later, and he would find her no matter where she was.

When she had heard that he had been asking after her in the village, she had fled in fear to St. Margaret's on the edge of the forest. And there he had found her. Of course, he had found her. He had dragged her out by her hair, dragged her over the roots and broken branches of the forest floor, and he had beaten and kicked her. Her and their child together. Then he had locked her in the tomb. And she had not fought back. She had known she had no chance of escaping what would now become her fate.

"Burn the heretic!" Tristan had shouted over and over to the people. "She has blasphemed God several times. I tell you, my ears have heard it clearly. Burn this godless woman and her devilish brat! Get on with it!"

For as long as she had held on to consciousness and the flames had not yet wholly taken possession of her body, she had not allowed her gaze to leave Tristan. And before she had slumped down, unconscious from pain, she saw that he had lowered his eyes in shame.

30

The vastness of time had vanished. Gone was any belief that countless days would string together and that death was a distant shore. Suddenly, time seemed to shrink to the duration of a few heartbeats.

Kathryn thought she could understand for the first time how a terminally ill person must feel. How they tried to savor the little bit of life they had left.

For a long time, only black or white had dominated her dreams. Now the other colors returned. In her dreams, she saw Freiburg with its houses spread out in front of her, which suddenly seemed extremely small. The lights in the houses seemed especially small. The lights with which people tried to defy the darkness. They had no idea what was coming.

Kathryn now knew the task that had to be accomplished. Knew about the battle of the Eight that would decide the fate of the world. Daniel and this powerful woman named Martha von Falkenstein, who had returned from a distant past, had told her about it. Although the whole thing sounded completely absurd, she did not doubt the truth of their words. Didn't doubt that something horrible was about to happen. Something that had to be averted at all costs. She felt it. The memory of the attack by the ghastly creature on the Martin Gate was too haunting.

Daniel had led Kathryn to a small clearing that lay in front of a chapel hidden deep in the Black Forest. St. Margaret's. In the moonlight, the landscape all around had glowed a fragile white. The other two were waiting there: Martha, and Zoe, who was only slightly younger than Kathryn, maybe seventeen. She had a dark complexion and looked quite athletic. She seemed well prepared for the task that lay ahead of them. Her dark eyes were shining. Her face was calm and seemed to glow with energy. With the saber she held in her hand, she looked like a born fighter. And she apparently was, as Martha reported. However, Zoe also seemed aloof. Suspicious. You could tell that she had already fallen into a few traps in her life. And that she had learned to carefully examine her surroundings.

Daniel told her about his love for the young woman named Isabel and that he had witnessed her murder. He told her about his brother Balder, who had become a monstrous creature. Kathryn told them about her encounter with the monster. About her dead love, the magpie, and the long dagger that looked like a bird's feather. The dagger that had magically appeared and saved her life.

She showed the dagger to Zoe. Handed it to her for a brief moment.

Astonished, Zoe held it in her hands, feeling the blade with her fingers. Something was tumbling around on inside her. The stories she had been told were having an effect. Her face opened up. Finally, hesitantly, she came out of herself. She told the two of them that she had also been having strange experiences lately. Dark thoughts. Perceptions. And that she had met him. Tristan Nightsworn. Had felt his violence. She told them that she dreamed of him.

Of his eyes, which were like a two-way mirror. You felt that you were being watched intensely, but you saw only one thing: your own reflection, cruelly disfigured. Zoe fell silent. Looked at Crow, then Daniel, then Martha.

"I will fight with you," she finally said. But her voice suddenly sounded weak. Sounded like dry leaves.

Crow turned to Martha with a question. "Guess the world doesn't know about the Fantastic Four fighting for them."

"No," she replied, "The eight chosen warriors fight the battle in secret. If our opponents win, the world will know it painfully. If we win, the world will have a new day. That's how it is."

Crow took a teensy bit of pleasure in teasing Martha, "No victory wreath, no money, no trophy? Not even a Spotify subscription?" Martha looked at her questioningly.

"You'd like that." Crow added, "I'm sure they have medieval music."

"I'm sorry," Martha finally said. "This fight won't win you any prizes."

Crow laughed. "Perfect. That sounds like the world I know. Worth fighting for any time."

Quite quickly, however, Crow's laughter faded again. Fear had taken root in her. In her previous life, she had always kept the doors to fear well locked. Now she was no longer able to do so. She doubted herself. Doubted that she would be strong enough to prevail in this battle. Also, a voice inside her whispered that she was not worthy of being one of the chosen few. Self-hatred flared up inside her. She had known it since childhood. She had never been a good friend to herself. For a long time, she had kept it a secret that she liked women. When she had opened up about it, the reactions had been terrible. All the critical voices, all the dirty looks, the violence she experienced, had begun to affect her. They had brought it out, that self-hatred. Until the night came when she almost killed that guy.

Almost? As she later learned, he had taken his own life some time ago. Lenny, his name was, had jumped in front of an Intercity Express Train. Depression, they said. He lay buried in Freiburg's parklike main cemetery. Just like Rebecca. This fact had filled Kathryn with anger. With a feeling of powerlessness. The feeling that one simply could not escape one's fate. No matter how hard one tried.

But then she learned from Martha and Daniel what was to come: They could be dead very soon along with every other human. The end of the world was very probably near. Kathryn could not stop thinking about it. She thought about what mattered to her in the time she had left. Suddenly a strange need arose in her. She made a plan. It was not difficult. She immediately found the name on the Internet. So she took the streetcar, Line 1. She went as far as the Landwasser district and walked to a three-story house covered with graffiti.

She rang the bell, and a woman opened the door of the first-floor apartment. Lenny's mother. Kathryn introduced herself to the woman. She said what she had wanted to say.

That she was terribly sorry for everything.

31

At Schleiermoos farm, in the small attic room he had shared with Balder, Daniel sat on his bed. He looked thoughtfully at the dark spot on the floor where his brother's bed had stood. His father had had Daniel's brothers remove it immediately after his release from the hospital.

Over the years, the afternoon sun that peeked across the dark mountains and through the small windows during the summer months had bleached the wooden floor, leaving only the spot under Balder's bed dark.

How will this end? Will I be able to defeat him in battle? My brother? The monster? The thoughts tumbled through Daniel's mind. They created images of a vicious fight. If Daniel emerged victorious from it—then, yes, perhaps the world would survive. A burden far too heavy for a weakling like him. Daniel stood up and stepped over to the dresser under the window. He opened a drawer and took out a small box. He flipped open the lid and carefully took out a few pictures, which he looked at in silence. One scene showed Balder and him on St. Martin's Day Eve when they had gone from farm to farm with lanterns. His face looked joyful in the lantern glow. Their songs reached him as if from far away.

I go with my lantern, and my lantern goes with me.
The stars shine up there; down here, along shine we!

Balder had loved that silly song. He had not stopped singing it, all night long.

Daniel felt his mouth go dry. His eyes fell on his Magnificat, which he had received at his first Holy Communion. It was in the very back of the open drawer. He took it out and sat down on his bed.

He began to pray, first to St. Mary, then to Jesus Christ. *Please let this cup pass.* In the middle of the prayer, he suddenly stopped and tore one page after another from the prayer book. Crumpled them up before hurling the book into the corner with an irrepressible force of anger.

Then he sat frozen on the edge of the bed for minutes, unable to believe what he had just done.

32

They found a way to her. Again and again. The doubts. The tormenting feelings of uncertainty. Martha could not escape them. She moved slowly through medieval section of Freiburg. It was evening. The uneven cobblestones beneath her feet reminded her of old, bygone times when death lurked around every corner. Today, tourists passed her way, and school classes from Alsace bustled through the narrow streets.

Were the three young companions she had chosen strong enough for what lay ahead? Had she burdened them with a task that was far too big for them? What would they have to endure? The horrors of battle, of death? Of doom? Briefly, she thought she foresaw it. The wild storm of the army of the dead sweeping through the air to take everything with it . . .

Dusk had fallen. Martha immersed herself in the small pedestrian quarter around Konvikt Street, where many craftsmen had had their homes in her days. The neighborhood had been called Wolf's Den, because the howling of the countless wolves could be heard at night, echoing from nearby Castle Hill. The picturesque alley, with its curving path, seemed today to radiate the warmth of peace. Martha paused in the sulfur-yellow glow of a streetlamp to collect herself. She knew how fragile that peace was. Thoughts of the army of the dead still beset her. She tried to focus again on her companions. On Zoe, on Daniel and Kathryn.

She opened her third eye, through which she could watch their every move. She saw the three of them just sitting together in the clearing in front of the chapel. They had lit a campfire and were roasting stick bread, joking around. They were making little jokes about Martha. Mimicked how earnestly she had spoken of the great importance of their shared purpose.

A smile crossed Martha's face. She was glad they hadn't let fear drag them away. Not yet.

She now saw Zoe teaching Daniel some saber fencing skills. The two faced each other, and Zoe performed slow-flowing movements that Daniel mimicked. Gradually it became clear that he was finding his rhythm. Only occasionally did Zoe point out that his weight was on the wrong foot or that he had left himself open for the killing blow.

Martha was touched by the bravery of her three companions. She felt all at once sure that she had picked the right ones. Perhaps they would succeed. Maybe they would prevail in battle.

Still standing in the light of the lamp, she sent her thoughts far back. Many centuries back. To the night before the great battle for Damiette. She thought of how she had slept with Tristan Nightsworn that night. She had known immediately afterward that she was pregnant. She thought of the rose that Tristan had given her that night. A special rose. It was called the Copper Queen.

33

He lingered in the dark depths in the great hall of Xanas Fortress. He sat on the stone seat. Half-ruined stairs led up to it, and it looked like a throne. Many of his ancestors had sat here. They had indeed been rulers. Rulers of darkness.

He could sense exactly where his companions were that night. They roamed above the surface of the water on land, celebrating a feast of carnal desire, of intoxication and blood and violence. A final feast with which they prepared themselves for the battle of the Eight. For the downfall. It was good for them to have their fun, exuberant, putting their senses to use. Their senses.

Their teeth. Their weapons.

Tristan Nightsworn had no desire to join them. He wanted to be alone. He gazed with heavy eyes into the vast empty hall, where water ran down its walls. The hall oozed rot and was as sunken as the past.

But the past rose briefly to him. The images, the perceptions that immediately followed his death so many centuries ago.

After the water of the lake had choked away his life, Tristan had come to as if just awakening from a horrible dream. He still felt the icy cold, felt the decay in his mouth, the burning in his throat. Deep inside him burned Martha's name. As loudly as he could, he had screamed it out. His screams had rung in his ears, but otherwise, all was silent. No one answered.

He coughed and coughed.

Despair had seized him. Sorrow at what he had done. Sending Martha, the woman he loved, into the fire. What he had destroyed. His whole existence had been one of annihilation. He had begged for Martha, pleaded into the silence for her to appear before him. But she did not. He groped his way along stone walls, finding himself in an inescapable labyrinth curved in the looping shape of the number 8. Again and again, he had followed the two curves that ran one back into the other. Exhausted, he sank to his knees. Then he heard a voice coming to him from a distance, heard his name. Exactly where the two arcs of the figure eight met, a passageway had suddenly appeared.

Tristan slipped through. Beyond it, a vast hall opened. He had hoped to find Martha there. But the hope was in vain. His footsteps were lost in the vastness of this hall. Nothing and nobody was to be seen. Cautiously he moved forward. The hall had seemed to be hewn out of solid rock, the floor made of rough stone slabs, the high, dully shining walls decorated with reliefs. Tristan studied at them. At first, they had seemed strange and forbidding to him, but then something had altered inside him. He had realized that these symbols and images belonged to religions and tribes, some of which had long since ceased to exist. Tristan was suddenly able to draw on an ancient deep knowledge that he had not possessed before. All the symbols, all the images flooded into him, sank into his soul. He could interpret and understand them. He saw that they all referred to one thing.

The number 8.

He had learned of the Octad of Hermopolis, an ancient Egyptian belief that before creating the world, eight deities had moved as elemental forces. He felt the eight arms of the Hindu god Vishnu, that spanned the world. He immersed himself in the imagery of the Etruscans, who had believed in eight ages of the world. Learned the symbol from the Mythras mystery of the ladder of seven gates through which a soul had to wander; at its top was the eighth gate that would set it free.

With difficulty, Tristan had moved forward. Images on the reliefs continued to seep into his innermost being. The signposts of the Eightfold path that led Buddhists out of the circle of existence into nirvana. He beheld the faces of the eight humans Noah had rescued on his ark. Heard the whispers of the ancient Gnostics who spoke of the eight spheres of heaven. Saw the repetition through time and across the world of eight as the number of the beginning, of the new birth. His skin had begun to tingle. His eyes had become heavy, so heavy. But he was unable to close them.

On and on, he had traversed the huge stone hall that had seemed neverending. He had thought he would collapse at any moment. Again and again, he had called Martha's name, had screamed out how he cursed what he had done. How much he wished to be with her.

Then he had come to a wide staircase, also carved out of solid rock.

At the top of the stairs, a vast, richly decorated octagon spread out beneath his feet, carved into the stone floor. Again he heard the voice. A female voice. Gentle, sweet.

Not Martha's, though it sounded similar. It was so similar. As if it was meant to torment him. The sound of it tore him apart inside. He felt Martha's nearness and at the same time, felt that she was beyond his reach. He had put an end to her life in a horrible way. Her absence was gruesome.

He left the octagon behind him. A staircase led down again on the other side, the stairs growing narrower and narrower as he descended. Finally, they ended in a rectangular opening, a gateway into . . . somewhere. His hair stood on end as he fixed his gaze on it. The voice that had called him seemed to come to him from the portal's unfathomable depths. Then it fell silent. Tristan stared on at the portal, felt a sinister pull from it. He was able to turn his gaze from it. Then the strangely lovely voice spoke again.

"You have been chosen to fulfill a task. When the time comes."

"Why should I?" he had heard himself ask.

"Because this is the only path that will lead you to her. Through the oldest of all bonds between people. The bond of victim and destroyer. The bond of life and death. You are committed to this path. You have chosen your role. There is no turning back!"

Tristan had hesitated no longer. Step by step, he had descended, until the dismal gate had taken him completely.

34

Another day was nearing its end. Time was running out. The west glowed in bright colors that gradually changed to deep purple and then faded into the blue of evening.

Martha von Falkenstein warily approached the great cathedral with its tower poking into the sky. She looked up at the windows of a small enclosure. There, in the Middle Ages, the tower guard had stood watch, equipped with a horn to sound the alarm and a fire lantern, to indicate the direction of any fire he spotted in the city. But some eyes remained blind to death-bringing flames.

Martha entered the nave of the cathedral. The dark hooded robe that enveloped her slender body made her look like a monk—a monk who might go in and out of the cathedral every day. Inside, service was being conducted. But she paid no attention.

She sauntered through the dim coolness, which was filled with singing and the lowing of the organ. Turning into the side aisle, she walked past the stained-glass windows toward the south choir entrance. She ducked into the darkness of a small vault that hid her from the rest of the church's visitors. There she found her objective: the large octagonal sandstone set into the floor. The stone that was a gate.

Martha bent down and ran her fingers along the edges of the slab.

Suddenly she felt a gaze sharp against her back. A voice reached her ear.

"You know what's behind it."

Martha winced. Without turning around, she said, "What's behind it will forever stay behind it." Tristan let out a laugh.

"And you're really sure of that?" he asked. "Your companions wouldn't even have been suitable for hauling cargo in the time we once knew."

Martha rose. Turned slowly to face him. Looked him firmly in the eyes.

"The time we once knew it no longer exists."

The grin on Tristan's face gave way to a hateful expression that contorted his narrow visage into a grimace.

"Yes, but you've seen it? You've seen it just as I have. How little has changed, after all. The weak still exist. And the brave, the strong, the relentless, who know how to move across the world. They march on the bones of the weak. How little has changed in all this time. Now, at last, after eight hundred years, we shall play out our destiny."

Unmoving, she stood facing him. Her eyes still held his hard gaze.

"You are a fine fighter," he said. "That much is certain. But your fellow warriors have no stand against my blood-thirsty comrades. I've unleashed their hatred. You will not defeat us on your own. You will be entirely too busy protecting your protégés."

"My so-called protégés," she said, "are fighters who can protect themselves. You will learn."

"Oh, yes—I will see," he replied. He pointed his long index finger at the octagonal stone that represented the gate that separated the realm of death from the realm of the living. The outlines of four beasts appeared again on the stone as if they had been waiting for this moment to be re-inscribed there by the invisible hand.

In the figures on the stone, Martha recognized Tristan and the three fighters he had gathered behind him. Four messengers of doom, recruited one by one in a coldly calculated bid to destroy all of life in one final battle. Martha pointed at the stone herself. Directly opposite the dark messengers appeared four figures in human form.

The beasts and the humans seemed ready to fight each other, just as Tristan Nightsworn and Martha von Falkenstein faced each other in the choir vault.

"So, the eight combatants are set," Tristan said.

"Tomorrow night, when the sextons close the gates, we will assemble here. And then it will begin. The battle of the Eight. The one that will decide everything."

His smile now took on a trace of warmth, even tenderness. As if he felt an intimate pleasure at the thought of the coming battle. He made a move to retreat, but just before he left the vault, he turned, and the old hatred shimmered in his gaze once more.

"One of your fighters has potential, though, I must admit," he murmured. "I'm curious to see if she knows how to use it!" Once again, his long finger pointed at the octagonal sandstone.

What happened made Martha shudder. Suddenly, the four beasts became five, and the four humans became only three. She was shocked. She quickly tried to regain control of herself. *I will not give up,* she thought. *Whatever happens, I will fight.*

She pulled her robe a little to the side so that Tristan could see the glimmer of her battle armor made from the blossoms of a flower, and understand what kind of flower it was: the Copper Queen.

Martha watched the expression on his face change once again. From unyielding just a moment before, his features suddenly seemed to soften. Tristan looked vulnerable. He looked at her. Briefly, he raised his hand, seeming to want to touch her. But then his fingers paused in the air as if they had come against against an invisible barrier. He looked at her—with a look as if from far away. He looked at her like a dead man staring into the open sky from the pit that had been dug for him.

"You know why I came back," he said. "You know I have no choice."

"It makes no difference," she said. "People only ever return someplace to find something that's lost. No one returns for something new. Do they?" The two looked at each other. Gazed at each other through the vastness of time.

"Until tomorrow," Tristan said.

Then he withdrew, disappeared into the dim light of the house of worship.

⌒

Martha, still thinking of Tristan and the pictures on the sandstone, strode toward the main exit. The service had ended. The last organ sounds had faded away into the general buzz of people also moving toward the doors. Her ears rang from the clanging of the Hosanna bell, which the people of Freiburg just called the Old Bell. Martha knew precisely how old it was: eight hundred years.

35

Neither the moon nor the stars appeared in the sky above the walls of St. Margaret's. Milky clouds of mist drifted over the damp earth, enveloping the figures of the four who had gathered in the clearing. Before them rose what looked like a giant creature wrapped in a somber gown that hung down in tatters. The old hanging tree, the beech under whose branches Martha, after her return to life, had again assumed her former form of a young woman.

Kathryn felt the hard pounding of her heart. She was excited. She knew that something extraordinary was about to happen. Martha had prepared Daniel, Zoe, and her for it. Had said that they should meet in front of the tree that night. It was the last night before the Eight would face each other. Martha had told them that on that night, they would truly become warriors.

Kathryn had walked here with Daniel. They had spoken very little the entire way through the forest. Daniel looked pale, as if the loneliness of loss had drawn the color from his face. Kathryn knew what lay ahead was especially sharp for Daniel. A fight against a monster that had once been his brother. His eyes seemed clouded.

They had walked deeper and deeper into the forest together, through impenetrable shadows where all was quiet.

Through undergrowth so thick that Kathryn had gone ahead to cut a path.

Suddenly she heard his voice behind her. "I'm sorry, Kathryn. I'm sorry I never came to see you when . . ."

"When I was in the loony bin," she finished the sentence. "The nuthouse. The psycho circus."

She continued on. "Don't feel so bad. Because the truth is, I wouldn't have visited myself either. Even now, I like to put off visits with myself for another day." She had wanted to say something more. To give him courage. But she hadn't known how to do it. So, finally, she said, "Remember that cab driver I ripped off? There's no way I could have pulled that off without you." A little laugh escaped him.

"What an honor," he replied.

Finally, the two had reached the clearing. Martha was already waiting. Kathryn was always spellbound when she came face-to-face with her. It seemed like the light of a bygone era shone through her. A feeling Kathryn otherwise only knew from museum visits when she looked at ancient exhibits from human history.

Then Zoe also joined them. She was so beautiful with her dark hair, proud nose, the thick brows, the fiercely set lips. Zoe radiated strength and determination. But a strange distrust of her had arisen in Kathryn, without her being able to put her finger on why. There was a restlessness in Zoe. Like a twitching finger on the string of a drawn bow.

"It's time," Martha said. She stood with her back to the tree and fixed her gaze on the three companions standing before her. Zoe, Daniel, and Kathryn. They had all brought their weapons. Senufo saber, sword, long dagger.

"The eight combatants have been found," she continued. "Tomorrow night, the battle of the Eight will be fought in the cathedral of Freiburg. One dawn and one dusk still separate us from it. There will be four of us, and another four will be our opponents. We know what defines them. It is death. We also know what we stand for. It is life. Right here and now, you will come into contact with both powers. You will experience what it means to die and what it means to be born."

Then Kathryn noticed something. The bare branches of the hanging beech, which drooped to the earth like a black rain, suddenly seemed to fill with light like a fire's embers. Something was happening under the curtain of branches, as if a portal had opened through which this light was streaming.

She looked over at Zoe and Daniel. Saw their eyes widen.

Martha said, "What awaits you behind those branches requires courage. But I know that the three of you will muster that courage. Who will be the first to dare?"

Kathryn felt for the dagger she carried in a leather sheath on her belt. She knew the dagger would give her strength. The folding knife she used to carry had always been destined to spill someone's blood one day. She knew it was the same with the dagger. And yet, there was a crucial difference. She would use the dagger to preserve something else. To save something. She had named the dagger Rebecca. She unsheathed it.

Holding Rebecca in her right hand, she walked forward. She approached the tree anxiously. She turned once more to Zoe and Daniel, to find support in their eyes. Then she took a deep breath and slipped between the drooping branches of the tree.

The ember-like light seemed to penetrate her. She had to close her eyes. When she opened her lids again, she saw a narrow house in front of her. It appeared to be burned out, with black-rimmed, paneless windows tha looked like gaping wounds. Cracks crisscrossed the facade like varicose veins. The door hung loosely on its hinges. Above the door, a word was carved into the old stonework: *Dukkha*.

There was nothing else to see except the house, which stood in a dark void. Not a breath of wind stirred. No sound could be heard. Silence reigned. Kathryn could not even hear her own footsteps as she slowly approached the house. A feeling came over her that the house possessed an aura of evil, that its walls were permeated with thoughts of vengeance and hatred. Kathryn forced herself to put one foot in front of the other. As she peered into the gaping windows, sounds suddenly returned, deafening. They went through her bones into her very marrow. She heard a jumble of voices. Screams that were no longer screams but howling. As if people were being doused with gasoline and burned alive.

Through the windows Kathryn saw all the wars and battles waged over the centuries. The images and sounds flooded over her. She was struck by a sudden deep knowledge of the causes and excuses and emotions that led to so many atrocities. She gain a knowledge about a myriad techniques of fighting, skills passed down from generation to generation and honed toward perfect in each iteration. She felt the potential and capabilities of humans—their outstanding ability to kill.

She felt sick to her stomach and sank to the ground. Everything was spinning before her eyes. With enormous difficulty, she rose again. She felt the urge to run away. But she knew she couldn't. She knew that she must go inside the house. Prepared for the worst, she went through the doorway.

Inside the house, there was . . . nothing. It was completely empty. No sign of the terrible events Kathryn had seen from the outside. Inside, the house seemed larger, more spacious. The air inside was mild, pleasant, almost sweet. The dim silence seemed peaceful, like the shade of leaves in a summer forest. And now, as Kathryn looked back out through the windows, she saw the reverse of the images of before. She saw what had come out of centuries of battles and wars. Saw how people cleared the debris, cleared new paths. Saw how they helped restore each other and, against all odds, against despair and powerlessness, tried again and again to create a new and better world instead. She felt the hope they gave each other, deep in her heart.

She left the dilapidated walls and found herself back in the forest. Zoe and Daniel were still standing in front of the hanging beech, waiting anxiously for her return. Astonishment appeared on their faces. Kathryn suddenly realized that she was now wearing a suit of battle armor that fit tightly against her body and shimmered like copper. It felt . . . great. As if her body had found a home. She smiled. She knew she was ready. Ready to fight, for her three companions, for herself. Ready to fight for all people.

Martha hugged Kathryn. Then she turned her bright eyes to Daniel and Zoe. "Who wants to go next?"

36

Zoe was asleep. She felt the hard cold of the floor—in her dreams.

They had decided to spend the last night before the battle together in the chapel. Martha had spread out a large woolen blanket. The four companions who would face death tomorrow lay on it, close together in front of the altar under the figure of St. Margaret of Antioch. Darkness surrounded them. The narrow stained-glass windows trembled slightly. The wind rubbed against the masonry.

Zoe thought she was awake, but in truth, she was already asleep.

In her dream, she was no longer in the chapel. She opened a door, stepped into Fynn's bright room in the shared suite. Sometimes she would sneak into that room to have sex with him. But often, she snuck in alone when Fynn wasn't there. She wanted to feel close to him. She would lie in his bed and breathe in his scent that clung to the sheet. But it was only perceptible there, this scent. Otherwise, his bedroom smelled like nothing at all, which Zoe always found a bit creepy. The room was always neat. Clean as a whistle. There was never anything lying around. The walls were a white that stung your soul. No pictures, no posters hung up. There was a small writing corner, always with an open notebook bound in leather. A fancy fountain pen lay on a blank white page. There was never a single word written on it. Above the bed hung a shelf with a few books on it. There was never a new book added. They were always the same: a world atlas; two cookbooks—*Meat: Commodities & Techniques* and *The Manor House Kitchen*; a decrepitly old edition of *Culinary Leaves*, a book about German naturalists; Ernst Jünger's memoir *Storm of Steel* about the First World War; a history of the Ku Klux Klan; Carlos Castaneda's *Journey to Ixtlan*; and *The Book of the Law* by the occultist Aleister Crowley.

Zoe wasn't sure if Fynn had read the books, but she assumed that he had. There was nothing unnecessary in Fynn's life.

Even now, in her dream, she found the books again. She was lying on his bed. The whiteness of the walls darkened, and her shivering suddenly turned into a feeling of heat. Sweat beaded on her forehead. Fynn's face loomed over her. He leaned down toward her and murmured, "You know you belong to me. You know our future. We belong together. Humans are being punished, just like they deserve."

His gaze bore through her. She thought of the little life that was in her womb. She wanted to protect it. But then Fynn let her taste the white snowberries. One by one, he let them drop into her mouth. She couldn't eat her fill of them. A new sensation grew. Strong. Unstoppable. She was no longer distraught, not horrified at the renewed feeling of wanting to destroy this seed of life. Just as she wanted to destroy herself. She wanted to forget herself. To be rid of forget her whole miserable life.

Suddenly a memory of her father surfaced. Before he had been with her mother, her father had had another family. Another child. A son. The son had been killed in a highway motorcycle accident when he was twenty-two. Zoe remembered the December morning when her father found out.

She had been there when the call came in. After telling Zoe's mother what needed to be said, he had looked at his daughter. His face looked the same as always, without the slightest emotion. Then he had looked at her mother again and said, "I wish *she* had died, not him."

In her dream, Zoe was still lying on Fynn's bed. His face still hovered over her. But then it transformed. Became the face of the man who had emerged from Lake Flint.

And she heard his voice: *Come to me!*

✑

Zoe stood in the cold of the night. Her sleeping companions seemed not to have noticed that she had woken up. Silently she left the chapel. Not even Martha seemed to stir.

Zoe couldn't help herself. She followed the voice through the Black Forest. In a clearing, she stopped, because for a moment, she had the feeling that someone was following her . . .

✑

She reached the shore of Lake Flint. Four figures in cloaks waited there for Zoe. One of them was Tristan Nightsworn, one of them was Fynn. The two of them approached her, took the saber from her.

"How wonderful that you came," said Tristan. "I knew you would choose us. Knew you were a good girl. A good, good, bad girl."

With deft fingers, together they pulled the copper-colored suit off her body. She let it happen. The suit dropped to the ground. As if molting an old skin, she stood naked in the glow of the moon, which was as white as the walls in Fynn's room. The light slid over her tightly hewn, athletic body, running down her back.

"Come on!" said Fynn, leading the way and wading into the water. Zoe followed him. It wasn't cold. The water enveloped her soft as silk as she finally dove down into the depths.

PART THREE

THE BATTLE
OF THE EIGHT

37

It had not been a good day for the sacristan of the cathedral. Today, of all days, when he had planned something extraordinary.

The gladioli he had bought for the early service that autumn morning had slipped out of his arms and fallen into a puddle. Because he was running late and couldn't get any other flowers, he had picked them up and tried to clean them in the sacristy. He had consoled himself with the fact that the light of God effortlessly overcame the dirt of life. But the archbishop, who was conducting the early service in person, had scolded him severely. Then the sacristan had also forgotten to place the bookmarks in the archbishop's Bible.

Later, in the afternoon, two students had thrown up in the cathedral. The sacristan had had to mop up the vomit, which was stained with red wine, and escort the class, along with their hysterical teacher, outside. The sacristan was in his mid-thirties, not much of an authoritarian, and the role of groundskeeper and sexton, which he always had to assume, particularly displeased him and at times overwhelmed him. Shortly after that, the one old guy had reappeared, shouting through cracked teeth across the nave: "God is a bastard son of a bitch! And you're a pack of rapists and liars!"

Sometimes the sacristan wondered if God saw him at all. Whether He realized how much he was trying to do for Him. How he tried to help preserve His dignity. He and his small team of colleagues who took the job in shifts had a lot to do. They had to cope with the vast flow of more than a million tourists every year. Mass had to be prepared three times a day, on some days four times. In addition, there were organ concerts and choir performances. The sacristans had to answer questions, give tours. Take care of the priests' vestments, provide prayer books and candles. They had to clean patens, monstrances, and chalices up-stairs in the treasury. In short: be in charge of everything. And again and again, they had to reprimand people who did not know how to behave in a sacred place.

He should not even have been on duty that day. But someone had called in sick, so he had to come in and, what's more, take on the entire day shift alone.

Therefore, the sacristan had decided to do something daring today. And, if he thought about it, for the very first time in his life.

He planned to secretly spend the night in the cathedral. He was tired of talking to people. He wanted to have a con-versation with himself alone in God's house for a change. God could, of course, also take part in it, provided that he wanted to.

The sacristan wanted to go down into the crypt to the tombs of the former bishops, to reflect, pray a little, feel the breath of the centuries.

His workday ended at a quarter to ten. Now all that remained was to lock the doors and extinguish the sac-ramental candles. That always hurt his soul a little as he thought of the many people who had lit them during the day and paid for them with coins, and the silent wishes and prayers and loss that had brought them there.

He was about to lock the southern, Lamb portal when he froze at a loud noise in the cathedral. A violent thumping made the stone slabs of the floor shake. Again and again, the sacristan felt the floor vibrate. Throbbing. It felt like an onslaught from the depths. The sound seemed to come from the direction of the southern choir entrance.

There were rarely any earthquakes in this area. The sacristan had felt a small one once. In his little apartment in the Stühlinger district, the cupboard he had inherited from his grandfather had trembled a little.

But now, in the dark expanse of the cathedral, the sacristan realized very quickly that these tremors were not an earthquake. The source was something else. Something threatening. He decided to get out of the church as quickly as possible. And run. He shouldn't have still been there anyway.

But the sacristan did not leave. He decided he had a duty to the cathedral, and especially to the Lord. He had to get to the bottom of what was happening.

His gaze swept the pale glimmer of the Martyrs' Window as he slowly approached the southern choir entrance. He felt hyperaware of the earth's gravity. The throbbing grew louder and louder, and he felt its increasing force. Finally, he stepped through the choir entrance and reached the place from which the tremors seemed to emanate—the octagon stone set into the floor. The sacristan knew his way around this building, knew about every figure in the windows and carving in stone, every flaw, knew every tiny crack in the walls. He could tell the time of day by where the light streaming through the windows struck the stone pavement of the floor. But never before had he noticed the strange image that was now visible on the octagon. It showed five creatures with hideous grimaces about to pounce on three people.

The vibrations became stronger and stronger. Without a doubt, something was hiding under that stone, trying to get out with all its might. A violent shock followed, causing the stone to shake.

The sacristan heard a voice behind him.

"Under this stone awaits some nice company for you! You can join them!" The sexton felt as if icy cold water was coursing through his veins. Slowly he turned around. Dimly, he saw a figure with a hood pulled low over its face. The next thing he saw was the flashing blade of a scythe hissing down on him.

38

Night had penetrated the mighty walls of the cathedral with ease and taken over the nave and transept, the center and side aisles, the diamond-shaped vaulted ribs of the choir with its wreath of thirteen chapels. It had consumed centuries-old figures of saints into its darkness. Only from the small but steadfast light of the sacramental candles did it recoil.

Daniel watched the flickering of those candles as he stood inside the tall, spread-out structure, waiting for the final battle to begin. The battle of the Eight.

The three had entered the cathedral through the Creation Portal on the north side. Martha, who had gone ahead, had touched the door with the tip of Aurin's blade. Without the slightest sound, the door had opened of its own accord. Before stepping inside, Martha had glanced over her shoulder at her two companions as if to make sure they were still at her side. Then she had looked up at the sky, where sat a reddish moon like a bloodstain on black cloth. Briefly, loneliness had gleamed in her eyes. Even fear. But then, in a calm, determined voice, she had said to the two teens, "Follow me."

Daniel had seen her graceful body tighten as she entered the darkness of the cathedral. Crow had followed her. Daniel was left alone. For a brief moment.

He had gazed fixedly at the portal through which he was to pass. The various doors through which he had passed over the course of his life had come to his mind. Doors behind which evil lurked, and those that brought good. He thought of the big sliding door of the cow barn. How often he had pulled it open as a little boy to play in the hay and let the cows lick him with tongues that were almost as long as his arm.

Then—perhaps for the very last time, he thought—the green spruce door had appeared in his mind's eye. With all its many scratches. The door behind which was the room that Daniel had shared with Balder for so many years. The room where they had made those lanterns—the last glowing lanterns of their childhood.

Then, as Daniel had stepped through the cathedral's creation portal, he had felt as if he were passing through all the doors of his life once again.

∽

Inside the church, Martha, Crow, and Daniel were immediately enveloped by the shadows. Back-to-back, they slowly moved toward the nave. Martha had impressed upon her remaining companions: they should stay close together as long as possible. She had explained, "It shrinks our attack zone. To the narrow area where our three bodies become one." At the same time, she said, the three of them should stay away from the walls so as not to be too easily cornered. Their drawn weapons gleamed faintly—Aurin, Rebecca, Beloved Brother. Their copper-colored battle armor glowed faintly in the darkness.

Daniel could not see the others, but he sensed that they were already there. That they were lurking in the vastness of the church. Their opponents. Who were superior to them, and not just in numbers.

He felt like he was no longer breathing oxygen but pure darkness. The armor stuck to his skin. The grip of the sword felt damp. He strained to listen but heard only the pulsing of his blood, which sounded fainter than the echo of the sea in a conch shell.

He sensed Crow's restlessness as well as his own. The restlessness seemed almost to consume them. Crow could barely restrain herself, wanted desperately to spring into action. But that was precisely what Martha wished to avoid. She wanted to tempt their opponents to strike first. She had impressed upon her companions to hold back as long as possible and wait for Tristan's attack and that of his allies.

"We will be bait," she had said. "Only when they move first will we attack. We must remain vigilant. The vigilance of the mind is the vigilance of the weapon. The ability to wait is the ability to strike."

Daniel tightened his grip on the sword. They had reached the center aisle when suddenly a whisper ran along the walls. Light streamed in through the stained-glass windows. It was on the north side, but it was a warm glow that made Daniel think of the rising sun. On the south side, a cool blue filtered through the windows. The two colors blended together, and the cathedral seemed immersed in strange shimmering water.

The attack from the other five came suddenly.

Daniel saw the blade of Tristan Nightsworn's sword Xanas glistening in the air like a sardonic smile. The long, narrow piste of the nave where Crow, Martha, and he stood tightly together became a swirling battle line.

The three of them formed the center of a hurricane of flashing swords, slashes, blows, and thrusts. Still, the three moved as one. Stayed close together. Parried the attacks. Some sword blows slid off their armor. Again and again, blades hissed ineffectively through the air. But Daniel felt that his strength was quickly weakening. He thought that it was getting harder and harder for the three of them to withstand the onslaught. The gaps between them grew larger and they spread slowly apart to meet the attacks.

Then, suddenly, it was chaos. He no longer knew what was happening around him. He heard the blades crashing into each other, but distant and dull, as if from behind a pane of glass.

A young woman closed in on him, with slow steps that expressed her superiority. Zoe. Her face was sallow, as if dusted with powder. She wore a long, sinister-looking cloak just like the four other fighters who had grouped to tear the world to death.

"Hello, Daniel!" she said. Hearing her voice was like feeling deep loneliness.

Daniel saw her temple veins strain as she stared at him. Then she rushed forward. The blade of her Senufo saber flashed. He jerked the copper sword up and managed to deflect the attack.

"Guess you've been practicing some more," he heard Zoe say. "It won't do you any good." She pushed him violently away and let out a laugh that sounded like shattering glass.

"You betrayed us!" he shouted. "You were our best fighter. And you betrayed us!"

Their last night came back to him. The night before the fight. The one they had spent lying on the blanket together in St. Margaret's. He had suddenly woken up and had seen at once that something was wrong. Something terrible. Then he had seen that Zoe was no longer with them and had run out into the night. The sky above him had been like the folds of a dark ocean. Daniel had guessed what Zoe was up to. If he was honest with himself, he had suspected and feared it all along. Then he had heard her footfalls, not far from the chapel. He finally caught up with her in a clearing. Tried to hold her back.

"There's no going back," Zoe had said. "When tomorrow comes, there's only one thing you can do: fight me. Fight well, dear, sweet Daniel!"

She was right, there was nothing else he could do. Zoe kept running, and Daniel stayed behind. With a feeling of despair.

He had learned from Martha. that there was something in Zoe's life that like was an abyss. A need that was something like love, but not. Daniel didn't understand how Zoe could do such a thing. To him, love had always seemed like something radiant, healing. He didn't understand how there could a love so twisted and mutated that it found its fulfillment only in death.

Yes, he had let Zoe go. But he had still followed her—all the way to Lake Flint. There, at a safe distance, he had seen everything that happened with the four figures who had received Zoe. One of them had been his brother Balder. Or rather, what Balder had become.

They had lost Zoe that night. She was now fighting for the enemy side. She was relentless and knew how to use her relentlessness. In the few seconds in which his memories had distracted Daniel, she knocked the sword out of his hand, which fell clattering to the ground.

"Are you disappointed in?" he heard her say. "There's no justice in this world. Why are you fighting for it?" Zoe grabbed Daniel by the throat and punched him twice in the face, making him feel like his skull was going to split. She hurled him across the stone floor. He crashed into the hard wood of the front pew. He felt as if the entire cathedral shook under the impact. He lay doubled over in pain as Zoe came closer and looked down at him. But before her saber Bougeotte could stab him, Daniel managed to roll away from the sharp tip of the blade, which struck only the ground. He scrambled to his feet and grabbed his sword. His heart was racing, and he felt every pulse throb through his body.

He tried to attack Zoe. But whatever he did, he failed to break through her guard. She saw through every feint—as soon as he tried a direction, she was already waiting for him. Sweat poured down his face and body. They were caught between the wooden benches, within reach of each other's weapon. Again and again, their blades crossed. Then he made a careless move, and she plunged the saber into his flesh a thumb's length below his collarbone. He cried out. When she pulled her weapon out again, it made an ugly sound, and he felt as if his insides were being pulled out with it.

He saw the blood-covered blade of the Senufo saber. His eyes went dim. He was about to faint. He struggled against it. Wanted to escape, but his mind had no directions to offer.

In pain, he tried to climb over the wooden bench. But he didn't get far. He collapsed and dropped his sword, which landed with a thud on the pew. Lying on his back, he stared at the distant dome of the cathedral, which shone with a strange glow of color. Then Zoe appeared in front of him, blocking it from view.

And he knew: now he would die.

But then her saber met steel. Martha's sword, Aurin. Daniel struggled to raise his head as Zoe let go of him to lunge at Martha. She drew Zoe into the long central nave of the cathedral, but not only her.

Martha was fighting three opponents at once. Against Zoe. Against the guy named Fynn. And against Tristan. Never did Martha's body offer any of them a steady target. Holding Aurin in both hands, she slashed at her opponents in circular strikes. She whirled in elegant circles, striking anyone who dared to come closer. Her blade whistled and sang.

Daniel had no idea where Crow was. He could hear her voice from afar in the vastness of the cathedral. Strained sounds of battle. But he wasn't sure whether he really heard her. He watched as his world, that world for which he had fought fiercely, wavered from sharp to fuzzy and back again. And then he felt as if he were floating above his own body, looking down at himself.

A young man approached his body where it was slumped between the wooden benches. Terrifying, with deep blue eyes. He wore a long coat. It was his brother Balder. As if in a feverish dream, Daniel looked down at them both. Saw what they had both become. He thought about how fate tore people apart again and again—despite their deep bond. Turned them into enemies. How often, the only possible path was to fight.

He saw the mighty black sword that Balder held in his right hand. Daniel knew: the hour had come in which he had to fight against his brother. This duty brought him back into his body. It gave him the strength he needed to take him on. A life force. When he opened his eyes, he hardly felt his wound anymore. He reached for his sword. When he opened his eyes, he was ready for his final meeting with his brother.

39

Henry B. Lindt approached the young woman called Crow. He saw that she appeared athletic. Muscular. Agile. She radiated willpower, with eyes that seemed to flash just like the long dagger she held. He could tell she wasn't shying away from this fight. That she would not hesitate for a second to kill him.

The two met in the south aisle. Henry's eyes were sharper than ever before. They saw so well that he thought he could see her blood circulating beneath the copper-colored battle armor, see the vulnerability of her body as well as her soul. He judged that he was superior to her—in terms of physique and fighting skills. In addition, there was the coldness that pervaded his soul, which he could certainly take advantage of.

Nevertheless, Henry B. Lindt sensed that something was off. In his fingers, clasping the handle of his rapier Battlelord, there was a throbbing. And in his mouth: a taste of blood.

The two did not take their eyes off each other. Each waited for their opportunity. In a flash, he thrust, but Crow repelled his attack.

Yes, without a doubt, evil had fully awakened in him the knowledge of all that was terrible, void, pathetic in the world. But what went along with it was the knowledge of the wretchedness in himself. He suddenly felt reminded of the boy he had once been. Rich, handsome, favored by accident of birth. Envied by others. But he always thought he didn't deserve that envy. His classmates were further in class along than he was. They were more approachable. More sympathetic. That shared much that had been withheld from him. They seemed to have talented hearts. That possessed one crucial ability: to love.

That's why he had always felt left out himself, had been weak, lost. This feeling had grown deep inside and had conjured up hatred. Hatred against all people. The desire to hurt them. The desire for cruelty.

But at that moment, when he faced the young woman named Kathryn in the cathedral, he felt only the little boy inside him. The bad little boy. Incompetent. Hopeless. Lonely.

Lonely—it was the last word that went through Henry B. Lindt's mind before Kathryn plunged her dagger into his stomach. Before his scream was stifled in a gurgle, and he collapsed like an empty shell.

40

As Balder moved toward Daniel, wielding the black sword called Mistilo, he sensed the song. It reached his ears as if from far away. A distance that seemed as sweet and hopeful as the song itself. The song was familiar to him, but he could not remember which one it was. He heard no lyrics. Not yet. Only the melody, as a humming. It evoked longing. Longing and sadness. He pushed those feelings back. He didn't want to hear the song. He tried to be deaf to it, though he needed all his senses to be alert at that moment for the fight.

He saw his opponent in front of him. He knew this was his brother. But that did not deter him. All that mattered was that he was Balder and he carried Mistilo with him, Mistilo's power bundled in his sword. A devastating weapon. He was now master of Mistilo, no longer at its mercy. He could use it purposefully. And he knew exactly what for.

Yes, the opponent might be his brother. But this brother had no chance against him. Even more, Daniel had already been injured by Zoe's saber.

Balder wasn't an idiot. He was not the idiot they had all always claimed he was—his father, his brothers, his classmates. The girls laughed at him, with their voices like silver bells and their hearts like granite: *Maybe you should do it with him! Stupid boys are good fucks!* Balder knew himself now. There was no longer any doubt. He was something special. Strong. He would help destroy them. The girls, their granite hearts. All those creatures out there who called themselves fathers, brothers. No matter what their names were. Their names would be torn from them. They would die . . .

If only there weren't this person in front of him, this face he now recognized more and more clearly in the mysterious light. Daniel. With his gentle eyes. That made it seem as if everything in this world had its place. Despair as well as love. A world to which you felt you belonged. Maybe a world that was worth fighting for?

No.

Balder would be strong. With Mistilo's black blade, he would shatter this mirage. And he would kill his brother.

Balder saw how hard it was for Daniel to stay on his feet. It would be easy to kill him.

And it was.

At first, the sharp black blade held back. Was almost gentle. It grazed the side of Daniel's head, taking only a nick from of his right ear with it. But then, it couldn't hold back anymore. It ripped his brother apart, tore him to shreds. The sword. The demon Mistilo.

Balder wanted to be close as he killed him. Very close. Wanted to watch Daniel breathe his last. He pulled his badly wounded brother up to him, so that Daniel half sat against him, half lay against him.

Daniel's bloodied lips opened one last time. Faintly, shakily, barely perceptible, and yet, it penetrated deeper into Balder's body than any blade could have. It pierced into his most hidden corners, branched out and flowed back to his heart—the song. When Balder heard his brother's labored words, he finally recognized it. And the song recognized him. Recognized the person he had once been:

I go with my lantern, and my lantern goes with me.
The stars shine up there; down here . . .

The song dissipated with Daniel's last breath. Balder uttered a cry of infinite pain. He picked up Mistilo and chopped off his own right hand, the hand that had killed his brother. It fell to the stone slabs in a torrent of blood. Then he straightened up and plunged the blade deep into his own body. To extinguish the last echo of the song. And to destroy the demon.

Balder's body slumped over, dead. The sword began to disperse. To become invisible. Mistilo fled into his lifeless body as if trying to find its own final resting place.

41

enry B. Lindt lay dead at her feet. It was the first time. The first time Crow had really killed a human being. She didn't like the feeling. The feeling of happiness. Of great happiness.

Crow wanted to charge on. Keep fighting. Help Martha and Daniel. But she couldn't. She felt utter exhaustion. Breathing heavily, she looked around. She had the strange sensation that the cathedral didn't really exist anymore. The walls had receded. She had the feeling of being outdoors in a hazy expanse in which the laws of space and time seemed to be suspended.

During the duel with Henry B. Lindt, Crow had heard strange things. She had heard the wailing of sirens. Heard the sound of bombs falling. Had felt detonations. Again and again, she had thought she saw the shadowy figures soldiers of long-past centuries, roaring into battle near her.

Even Henry's dead body seemed to her like a corpse lying in the dirt of a battlefield. Despair surged over Crow. She remembered how she had felt that morning. When she had learned from Daniel and Martha that Zoe would not be fighting by their side but was now their foe. In the chapel, Crow had knocked over the brittle baptismal font, which had crashed to pieces. She had been horribly angry. Disappointed. But above all, she had lost her courage which she had so laboriously awakened. She had felt as if the ground beneath her feet were slipping away. Three against five—a challenge that could not be overcome. Kathryn had no longer believed in the three of them. Not in herself. Not that she would ever see another dawn. Just as she no longer believed in it now.

But Martha's words came to her. Martha had talked to Daniel and Kathryn. The words gave Kathryn support. They brought back the space she was in right now, a solid place in which she could orient herself. Her words whispered themselves into Kathryn's ear, as if echoing softly off the walls of the monumental structure.

Yes, we may be defeated by these five opponents. But don't let your thoughts defeat you before that. Sometimes it is not the events themselves that are the most terrible thing. What is terrible are our thoughts about them. I understand that you're thinking: there are only three of us. But that is belittling what we should be strengthening: ourselves. However many we number, that will not change the attitude with which we face our opponents. Unless we allow it to.

No, we do not know what fate awaits us. Yes, we have lost people, we have lost comrades, we have lost hopes. But as the three of us come together here, we are one thing: complete. We are not lacking in courage.

We lack nothing we need to fight for this all-important cause.

Crow felt herself gathering strength once again. She tightened her grip on the long dagger whose blade was stained with blood. She ran to help Martha in her fight against Tristan, Zoe, and Fynn as quickly as she could. She managed to push her way between the opponents and keep at least Fynn away from Martha by taking him on herself. Again and again, he tried to hit Kathryn with his scythe. But she dodged him in time, each time. Then she managed to knock the weapon out of his hand with a lightning-fast upward movement. She tried to stab at him, but Fynn reflexively pulled in his stomach, and the blade cut only air. He reacted immediately, yanking her to the ground. He threw himself on top of her, tried to get a grip on the dagger. He caught her arm as she continued to stab at him in vain. Kathryn didn't know how long they wrestled. Fynn was a lot stronger than she was. It was getting harder and harder to hold on to the sweaty hilt of the dagger.

He clamped her hand under one arm while he thrashed her face with his free fist. She felt herself slowly sinking into darkness. Felt her grip on the dagger loosen until it landed on the floor with a clattering sound.

Fynn straightened and yanked Kathryn up by her hair. Again and again, he struck her face with his fist until she went limp and could only just barely keep herself on her knees. Calmly, he picked up his scythe Forget-Me-Not. Behind her swollen eyes, deep in her subconscious, she thought she perceived for a moment the flutter of bird wings in an opening sky. Then he sliced off her head.

42

She was an excellent swordswoman. Still. Or again. Whatever you wanted to call it. Martha von Falkenstein was difficult to defeat. Tristan Nightsworn realized this quickly. With a feeling of admiration.

She had learned some of her skills from him. But initiation into the art of fighting had hardly been necessary with her. Even before they had met for the first time, Martha had fought her way forward, through night and day.

She had taken on opponents the daughter of a poor, sickly maid should not have been able to defeat. Martha had run away at great risk, to go to war with him.

Only many years later would she return to her home village, which had been burned down in the meantime. She returned, scarred by the battles. But within her, she had the beginning of life. Her mother had long since been carried off by the plague. Only her little sister Keth had survived. But she, too, was to fare badly after Martha's death. Tristan had learned her fate while he himself was still alive. Keth had been raped and hanged by bandits who had raided the village.

Now they were face to face. Martha and himself. In a completely different time than when they had loved each other. Long since dead and now come back to life. Martha had first knocked Fynn, then Zoe, to the floor. They both lay on the stone slabs, writhing. Groaning. Marked. Bright red seeped from their wounds. They were no longer her opponents now.

Tristan felt the glimmer of Martha's battle armor like a longing. A longing that needed to be conquered. He looked into Martha's face. He saw the blood running down it, starting from her forehead, down her right brow, her cheek, to her chin, where the drops beaded and dripped off. He saw her determined eyes. He thought of what a great feeling it had once been to fight side by side with this woman. Undaunted, she had thrown herself into every battle. Now they were enemies. Now he had to take her on. It would be the last fight for them both. She had Aurin raised, ready to strike. He felt a soundless vibration emanating from Martha's blade, which was echoed and multiplied in Xanas. He felt that the two swords belonged to each other. That they called to each other, like two voices in the deep darkness.

Xanas flashed and drew a deadly arc, but she was able to parry the attack. Sparks flew up as the blades clashed against each other. Then he felt a silence envelop them both. A silence like that of the cold universe, where suns had been extinguished for ages. They circled each other. Then out of the silence came the whirring. The whirring of Aurin's blade. He heard it even before her attack came.

He intercepted her blow. He struck back without breaking through her defenses. On and on, they fought. Driving each other through the nave. Her eyes stayed locked on his as they jumped back and forth, and the attacks surged back and forth. A dance emerged from their struggle. Step,

attack, parry, step. He felt the closeness of her body. He felt
her breath, which quickened, followed by his like an echo,
until he could no longer distinguish between them. Faster
and faster their breathing became. Faster and fiercer came
the strokes, while their feet made a rhythm of their steps
as if on their own.

Until a memory broke through.

For weeks the crusaders had been trying in vain to confront the main army of the Sultan al-Adil, which had deftly
eluded them time and again. The Crusader army, of which
he and Martha were a part, had been slowly worn down.
Demoralized and weary, the men had pitched camp on a
hill not far from the Sea of Galilee. Tristan had not been
as weary as the others. For no matter how hard and deso-
late those days under the alien sun turned out to be, luck
had remained steadily on his side. And it bore the name of
Martha. Tristan could well remember the sight of the lake
when night gradually fell. The unusually cold wind that
had blown across the water. In front of the tent, they had
lit a meager campfire. With bodies pressed close together, Tristan and Martha had danced around the fire to the
sounds of the wind, to sounds only in their imaginations.
Above them, a rose-colored sky was slowly consumed by
darkness. The sparks of the fire shot up into the night
air.

By the time the memory faded and he realized where
he was again, Martha had knocked Xanas out of his hand.
They came to a stop, and Martha placed the tip of Aurin's
blade over his heart.

"This is where I leave you for good, Tristan," she murmured to him.

Martha pushed the sword into his heart. Tristan felt as if the blade was made of flame. The fire ate deep into him, into his core, until there was only a blazing hiss that swelled into a roar.

The roar of the fire that destroyed him.

43

Martha von Falkenstein was the last. The last one left of the allies who had stood against the downfall of the world. She could feel the pain building up inside her. She had seen it in her dreams. Over and over again. But in all her dreams, she had not been the last one. It was someone else. She had never been able to make out which of the eight fighters it was. The figure in her dream was, unclear, its face flooded with light. The face had never shown itself. But Martha had always woken up with a deep feeling of happiness. For she had clearly felt that this figure in her dreams would prevent the downfall of the world.

Now she knew that the truth was different. The pain inside her turned into despair. They had all died violent deaths—everyone who had helped her since her return to this life. First, the old man Christian Albert, the dog Nina, Isabel, Daniel, and Kathryn. They were all dead. Not a single one of them had been able to save her. They had died only because of her. She felt shame. She didn't think she deserved to be the one survivor. She had failed. She could barely go on holding Aurin in her hand.

The sword suddenly seemed to have enormous weight. For the first time, she also felt the injuries her body had sustained in the battle of the Eight. She felt her armor hanging down in tatters on one side. What was left of it was soaked with sweat. And blood.

Martha heard a thumping that accompanied a shaking of the ground—the onrushing army of the dead that had formed and was about to be released. All life would be destroyed. If Martha did not stop it.

Suddenly she saw a figure dressed in a dark cloak. Closer and closer it came, holding a scythe in its right hand. Zoe was still curled up on the stones, but Fynn had gotten back to his feet. He, too, was covered in blood. Still, she could feel his strength. His tense muscles seemed to almost rupture the skin of his body.

There was no emotion on his face. No fear. Nor the ferocity that could burst from him at any moment. Forget-Me-Not looked like a frozen flame from hell. Martha felt its coldness. She felt a fear that seemed to paralyze her limbs—the fear of failing again. Blood still seeped into her eyes, seemed to show her more strongly than ever the world as it really was. The world through which her soul had roamed far beyond death. What had this world for which she was fighting given her? Pain, violence, frenzy. It had given her a homeless loneliness. An eternal song of hunger. Wars. Battles. And a fleeting breath of love that could not be saved.

Cannot be saved? Martha tried to gather all her strength. *You must be strong,* she told herself—*one last time. You don't know what can be saved. But you know what is worth saving.*

Ponderously, the two moved toward each other. As if they had to climb over a field of rubble to face this confrontation. With both hands, she brandished Aurin. As their weapons clashed, stars flashed before Martha's eyes. Then, with the next blow, she felt the scythe blade bite deep into the flesh of her left shoulder. Red blood gushed forth, and blackness surrounded her. A terrible weakness overcame her, and Martha felt the urge to let herself sink to the ground. But she resisted, staying on her feet. When she raised her eyes to look at her opponent again, she saw that Fynn had two weapons in his hands. In his right hand, he held the scythe. And his left hand grasped Xanas. His mouth twisted into a callous smile. She felt how strong this opponent was. A destructive force emanated from his cold heart. But Martha would take him on. She was still here. She was still standing. She stretched Aurin aloft, ready to strike.

Her blow was intercepted. Fynn returned it, and Xanas struck her left knee with a hiss. Martha tumbled to the ground, and Fynn threw himself on top of her. Again she saw the ice-cold smile on his face.

"Isn't this great?" she heard him say. "My face will be the last thing your nasty little world sees." He put Xanas' blade to Martha's neck and slit her throat.

44

Zoe was still lying on her back on the cold floor of the south aisle.

Pain raged like a noise in her head. Penetrated all the way to her guts. Like Martha's blade, which had slid between her ribs during the fight.

Zoe felt the pain and the pool of her own blood in which she lay.

When she opened her eyes, she saw a glint of the sort of sunlight she only knew from Mali. The land of her ancestors, which looked like a butterfly flying at an angle on the map. Her mother had been born in Sikasso, a town in the south. Later, she had returned there, seriously ill, to die. That had been her last wish in life. After her mother's death, Zoe had traveled the country for a few weeks. Had visitied the semidesert of the Sahel. In the shimmering sunlight, she had seen the salt pits of Taoudenni from afar. She had met nomads who transported large sheets of salt through the desert on their camels. In the north, she had made excursions into the Sahara and had seen the mosque of Djenné towering under the steel-blue sky, the largest adobe clay mosque in the world.

Zoe loved that country. When she was a girl, her mother had said to her, "It will never be too close and crowded for you out there in the world. For under your skin will always be the vastness of the desert." But Zoe often forgot it: the vastness beneath her skin.

But now, lying wounded on the cold church floor, that strange glint of light entered her eyes, and the desert briefly returned. Then the light suddenly disappeared.

When Zoe emerged from her stupor, everything was gray around her in the vast cathedral. It appeared as if wisps of mist were creeping across the floor and enveloping her body. A face looked down at her. It was smeared with blood. She knew it well. It stretched into a triumphant smile.

"We did it," Fynn said. "Ace of spades and me, just the two of us. No one else." He reached under her armpits and helped her to her feet, then picked up Bougeotte and handed it to her.

"They're dead," he said. "Every last one of them. And rest of the world will be too, soon. Come on!" Fynn pulled her with him through the billowing mists, toward the southern choir entrance. As their footsteps echoed off the walls, Zoe noted the silence around them. A silence that still held close all the screams of battle. Though the veils of mist made them unrecognizable, Zoe sensed the blood-soaked corpses in that silence.

She felt the slashed cloak she wore on her body. On her hand, she felt the greasy blood clinging to the handle of her Senufo saber. She heard the eerie, the mighty rumbling of the army of the dead, growing louder. Louder and louder.

The two of them stepped through the choir entrance and reached the octagon outlined on the floor. Zoe had never seen it before. Looking down, she saw a depiction of two monstrous creatures facing each other. They stared at each other with ugly grimaces. Zoe glanced at Fynn. He was holding the two swords now, Aurin and Xanas. The swords that were to be united.

"Now, we finally fulfill our promise," he said. "We'll find each other again in the darkness, you and me, like these two blades." He brought the blades together. When they lay exactly on top of each other, it seemed all at once as if two disembodied souls were wrestling with each other. Fynn's hands began to tremble. Then, hissing, the two swords fused together, shrank together. And what emerged from their joining was a plain, slightly shiny key, radiating something . . . awe-inspiring. Fynn grinned.

Holding the key in his fingers, he knelt in front of the octagon. Like a fleeting shadow, the curve of a keyhole now loomed there. Recalling Tristan's instructions, Fynn whispered to himself, "Clockwise, the gate will be locked forever. Counterclockwise, it will be opened." Fynn looked up once more at Zoe, who—Bougeotte in her hand—stood beside him.

He said, "We'll dance, ace of spades. We'll dance a dance of death. Everything outside these walls—the whole world—will dance with us. If we free the army of doom. Do you feel it? Can't you feel it beginning? The dance?" The octagonal sandstone began to tremble more and more violently. Zoe felt a frightening throbbing that made the entire cathedral shake. Louder and louder it droned, stronger and stronger the vibrations grew. It seemed to Zoe that the sounds turned into music.

She thought she heard it. The dance. Its strange gliding beat. She needed to surrender to it, completely and totally. She felt death. Its sublimity. Its power to take over everything. And in her arose a feeling of happiness to be able to participate in this power. Even more, to be a part of those who unleashed it. All her thoughts, all other senses seemed to evaporate until only a rigid sinister will reigned within her, focused on a single goal: annihilation.

But then Zoe sensed something else. A movement, little more than a shiver. Out of the corner of her eye, she saw a small figure crouching in the shadows of the old masonry. When the figure moved forward a little, Zoe recognized the face. It was a child's face. The sad face of the child she had met on the deserted street in Günterstal. Then a second child's face appeared, and a third, until in every niche, every corner, from behind every pillar of the cathedral, a child emerged. It was like she could see every face at once. She heard the voices of the children, each echoing the others, all shouting, as if in a chorus, the same sentence: *Where can all us children play?*

Zoe felt something stirring inside her, responding to the chorus of voices. She felt something change inside her.

Fynn sank the key into the keyhole of the octagon. He was about to turn it when he paused in surprise. The image on the stone had changed. There were no longer two monstrous creatures on it. Instead he now saw only the delicate outline of a single human being.

Confused, he looked up at Zoe, saw Bougeotte's blade pointed at him. He heard her voice, hard and decisive.

"Guess what?" she said. "The ace of spades is the high card today. The last card, that stands for life."

Fynn stared at her. How many times had he made people scream. How many times had he been the one to give out pain. It seemed now that there was not a single scream left for himself. His mouth opened. But he made no sound as Zoe rammed the blade of her saber deep into his body. His eyes went out. His face collapsed. Death came quickly. Fynn's heavy body fell to the ground. The octagon looked like a drawing over which red ink had been toppled.

∽

Zoe sealed the gate of doom. As she gently turned the key clockwise, the roar beyond it died away, and the gate sank as if into quicksand. Then the octagon itself disappeared as if it had never been there at all, only the plain stone floor left behind.

She breathed. And breathed. Leaning on her saber, she knelt, alone in the vastness of the cathedral, her head bowed.

Zoe felt it. The whole wide world out there. Felt mornings settling on thresholds and evenings lost in the branches. Zoe heard thunderstorms slapping against wild rock cliffs. And voices singing songs. She saw the people, the fleeting flowers of their lives. Their paths. Each one was a path home, for some woman, some man. Some child.

And when, after a while that seemed interminable, she lifted her eyes, light streamed through the cathedral's colorful windows in a luminous flood.

MY THANKS GO TO:

Knut Reinoss and the entire team at Arctis/Atrium Verlag. Ulrich Störiko-Blume for opening doors. My parents Jutta and Andreas, and my brave sister Lilly for their support from near and far.

The extended Koch family, always—fixed stars of Menz and Hossingen.

Steffi and Burak, who are even more significant in life than Maxe, Belle, and Soacher.

The wonderful Marohn family (including Daniel, of course) in their thoroughly reserved enchantment.

. . . as well as many friends and companions who could not reach me in the communications dead zone of the deep Black Forest for far too long.

Benjamin Lebert, born in 1982, has published seven novels, including his first novel *Crazy*, which has sold over 1.2 million copies, has been translated into 33 languages, and has been successfully adapted into a movie. The author is a founding member of the Lübeck Literature Meeting started by Günter Grass. Having grown up in Freiburg im Breisgau in the southwest of Germany, he has been hearing the myths and legends of the Black Forest since his childhood. Benjamin Lebert lives with his family in Hamburg.

Translator **Oliver Latsch** spent the first six years of his life in Zambia and Kenya, before moving to Hamburg, Germany. He studied ecology and conservation at the University of Sussex and completed a PhD in ecology at Imperial College in London. He lives with his family in Los Angeles, California.

INTERVIEW WITH
BENJAMIN LEBERT

Twenty years after publishing your first novel, *Crazy*, when you were only sixteen, where did you get the idea to write another novel about and for young people?
A while ago, I was traveling in Norway on a little reading tour. Among other things, I read at a school in a tiny snow-covered town called Ski. I talked to students from age fifteen to seventeen about literature, and about how it is possible to discover your very own narrative voice among all the voices that whisper within each of us—to approach the brave task of writing a story. But our conversations were also about longings and desires. I asked them to share some of those desires with the group if they felt like it. One student said, "Honestly, I only have one wish. Before I'm dead, I want to make this world know that I exist." Those words—simple and straightforward as they were—touched me. Because they glowed with so many things. Dream and reality. The enthusiasm of new beginnings. The fear of being a shooting star that burns up unseen in the dark. In that classroom, the student's words brought back to me—illuminated by the white light of the snow—the faintness, the despair, the loneliness of teenage life. At that moment, I felt the need, almost two decades after the publication of *Crazy*, to write another book for teenagers. This time from the point of view of a thirty-something—ancient!—man,

but with the desire to get as close as possible to young people. I wanted to write a book that would take young people seriously and ignite a little light for them, in hope of the best-case scenario that any of my sentences can do so at all. That is why at the beginning of the novel, which took shape in me over time, there is a scene in which a small candle is lit in a gloomy chapel. But already in that scene, the abyss is palpable. There is already a first hint of what fate will befall the young woman.

What attracted you to the fantasy genre?
In my opinion, dreaming oneself away into other spheres and spaces and longing for them is stronger in young people than in adults. And also the urge to cross borders—especially from the real to the unreal—and a specific sensitivity to things that take place in the shadows, things that cannot be seen with the naked eye. That's why it was imperative to me to incorporate fantastic elements into my new novel. The characters in the story are exposed to these fantastic happenings, have to position themselves against them, and grow from them. Since I was born in Freiburg and grew up with the sagas and legends of the Black Forest, I immediately knew what the incidents in the novel would grow out of.

Moreover, I am a hopeless dreamer myself, but one who, alas, will soon have to file his tax return . . .

As for the genre question: I know that it has enormous significance in art and entertainment. And rightly so. Assigning a genre helps to orient oneself. One knows immediately where one stands. But to be honest, I'm not the least bit interested in this question when it comes to writing. After all, our lives can't be assigned to one genre: drama, comedy, a fairy tale. Our life unites all narrative forms. At best, writing should do the same.

Sign of the Eight is about the struggle between good and evil, which also divides couples and families. What role do you think these categories play for today's young people?
The question of good and evil is primarily a question of nuances. Minimal stirrings—shifts, as it were—can make the difference that creates something ghastly, violent. In my previous novel, _The Darkness Among the Stars_, set in Nepal, I wrote about the lives of children. This time, it's about the lives of teenagers. What they have in common is how passionately they surrender to the big questions of life. How they don't want to avoid them.

On the contrary, in their innermost being, they want to sense these questions. Track them down, so to speak. That is why they are perhaps particularly vulnerable to whispers of any kind. Their senses are constantly aware of the forces that want to drag them back and forth. How young people deal with these forces, resist them or use them for something good, and in the process gradually begin to believe more firmly in their own power, is what _Sign of the Eight_ is about.

You once said about your new novel, "When I was a teenager myself, I would have liked a novel like this." What did you mean by that?
When I was a teenager myself, fantasy books were frowned upon and considered of dubious quality. The Harry Pot-

ter novels had not yet been published, and even The Lord of the Rings, the ivory tower of fantasy literature, had not yet been made into Peter Jackson's film adaptation, which conquered the whole world. The so-called realistic books for young people that we read in high school were strangely conservative. They seemed patronizing, since they strenuously excluded the true horror of youth. I did not find myself in them one bit. A small exception was *Rumble Fish* by Susan E. Hinton. So were *The Center of the World* by Andreas Steinhöfel and the great stories and novels of Joyce Carol Oates. Adult books and stories that explored being young, such as "Barn Burning" by William Faulkner, *The Red Pony* by John Steinbeck, *Paddy Clarke Ha Ha Ha* and *The Commitments* by Roddy Doyle, or even *Dzhamiliya* by Chingiz Aitmatov, didn't find their way to me until years later. Wonderful books for young people like *Tschick* by Wolfgang Herrndorf were written years later. That's why I felt pretty lost myself in a sad wasteland of literature, which tended to reinforce my generally perceived loneliness. I longed for a book that would combine many things: actual events, inexplicable phenomena, dreams, premonitions, desires for escape. I did not want to leave out despair and the abysses of youth, nor powerful natural wonders. One must not ignore them. One must perceive them. Experience them. You can only meet them with the power that is available to you. More is not possible. One's own ability that, in the best case, is perhaps love.

Are there also actual events and backgrounds that play into your book?

My grandfather comes to mind, who took me to the depths and heights of the Black Forest when I was a little boy. For example, Lake Mummel, one of the old basin lakes, dates back to the Ice Age. It lies on the slope of the Hornisgrinde and stares into the sky like a mysterious shimmering eye. It is the subject of many legends and tales. One legend, for example, particularly captivated me. It is about a forester's son who was eighteen years old and whose name was Berwin. One July evening, while sitting alone on the shore of Lake Mummel, Berwin saw a mysterious creature in the form of a magically beautiful woman emerge from the depths of the water. She came close to him and looked at him with her mysterious dark eyes. But before he could exchange a word with her, she disappeared again into the lake. All that remained of her was a delicate, gossamer veil, which Berwin took and guarded like a treasure. Henceforth he sat perpetually under the shining sun or under the sparkling moon at the water's edge and waited for the creature to return. As the longing ate his days, he became thinner and thinner. His cheeks paled and sank in. His parents, relatives, and friends spoke of an evil spirit that had befallen him. But he did not care. He didn't care about anything anymore. His eyes gazed on, continued to stare at the shimmering water. Finally, in a fit of anger and despair, he threw the veil into the water. But quickly, he deeply regretted it and waded into the lake to find it again. But, of course, he did not find it. He only found death . . .

Stories of this kind still affect me today and strongly influenced my work on this book. But I am already drifting into the fantastic again. There are also everyday events that found their way into this story. For example, I once saw an old foreign man almost beaten up by two young people in a Freiburg streetcar. As they got off, I saw the bright eyes of one of them and heard his voice still telling the old man, "You're lucky, damn lucky, I tell you!" Those eyes and that voice were with me when the character named Fynn appeared in my novel.

Some descriptions in the novel actually correspond to actual events. For example, in the nineteen-thirties, a group of English youths really did get caught in a snowstorm on the Schauinsland—which meant death for some of them. It is also true that in the Middle Ages, in times of need, it often happened that hungry adults lured away small children and then ate them. In general, I want to make it clear that the thing that could be called "evil" in the world is very voracious. It can only revive when weak beings unable to defend themselves against it are consumed.

In other descriptions—certain places, characters, events—I have taken narrative liberties. If someone should set out to find Lake Flint in the Middle Black Forest, he or she will probably not find it. Likewise, St. Margaret's Chapel. But who knows? Maybe they will be surprised. I believe that we should train our eyes for the invisible. Legends and myths, including those of the Black Forest, are often based on a kernel of truth. Since these are alluded to in this story, it was important to me to live up to them insofar as I gave free rein to my imagination, starting from an actual event, a place that actually existed, and so on.

Are there parallels in your novels, despite all the differences?

What all my books have in common is the look toward the sky. In my stories, people are always looking up there. Because, for me, the main reason people don't know what heaven has in store for them is that they look at it far too rarely.

How has your writing process evolved over two decades?

I don't particularly like the term "evolve." Because it suggests that a distance has to be traversed. But for me, life is less about spaces and more about closeness. I want to get close to people. Even if it's sometimes tricky, it's an important endeavor. In writing, too, I want to create closeness to characters, but also to an unknown person sitting somewhere out there opening a book.